Maya

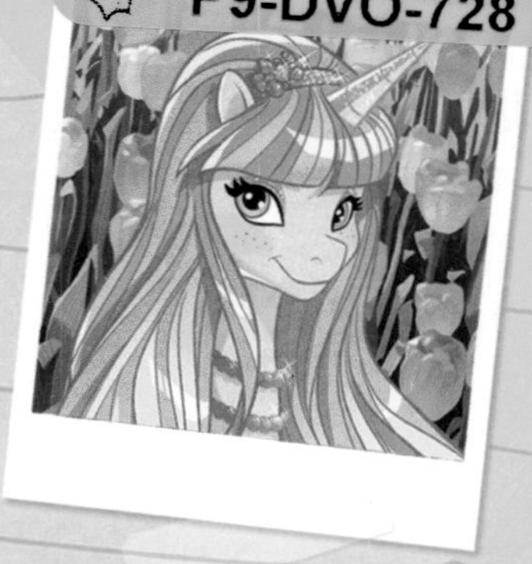

Her realm: Spring
Her personality: shy and sweet
Her passion: cooking
Her gift: the Power of Heat

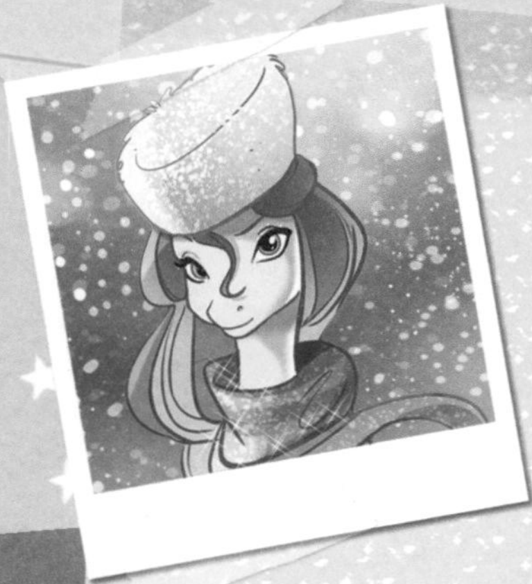

Cora

Her realm: Winter
Her personality: proud and sincere
Her passion: ice-skating
Her gift: the Power of Cold

Selena

Her realm: Night
Her personality: deep and sensitive
Her passion: music
Her gift: the Power of Darkness

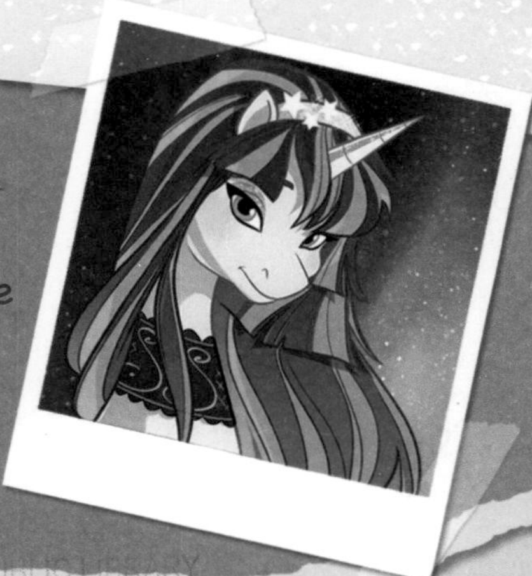

MELOWY

PAPERCUTZ

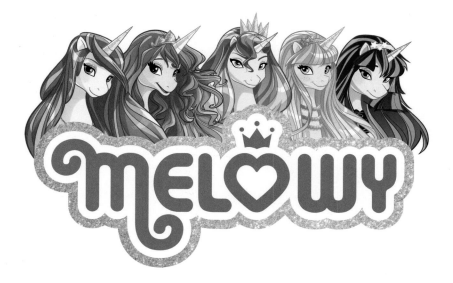

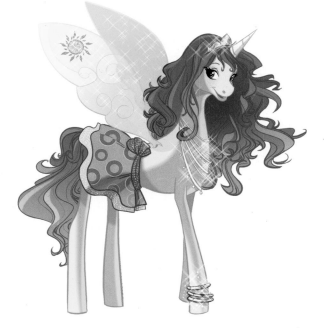

MORE GREAT GRAPHIC NOVEL SERIES AVAILABLE FROM PAPERCUT2

THE SMURFS 3 IN 1 #1 — **TROLLS 3 IN 1** — **THEA STILTON 3 IN 1 #1** — **GERONIMO STILTON 3 IN 1 #1** — **THE LOUD HOUSE 3 IN 1 #1**

GEEKY F@B 5 #1 — **DINOSAUR EXPLORERS #1** — **MELOWY #1** — **MANOSAURS #1** — **SCARLETT**

ANNE OF GREEN BAGELS #1 — **DRACULA MARRIES FRANKENSTEIN!** — **THE RED SHOES** — **THE LITTLE MERMAID** — **FUZZY BASEBALL**

HOTEL TRANSYLVANIA #1 — **HOTEL TRANSYLVANIA #2** — **HOTEL TRANSYLVANIA #3** — **THE ONLY LIVING BOY #5** — **GUMBY #1**

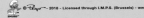

© Peyo — 2018 - Licensed through I.M.P.S. (Brussels) - www.smurf.

The Fashion Club of Colors

Cortney Powell — Writer
Ryan Jampole — Artist
MELOWY created by **Danielle Star**

PAPERCUT**Z**
New York

MELOWY #2
"The Fashion Club of Colors"

Copyright ©2018 by Atlantyca S.p.A. Via Leopardi 8, 20123
Milano, Italia. – foreignrights@atlantyca.it
© 2018 for this Work in English language by Papercutz.
All rights reserved.

Melowy created by DANIELLE STAR
Cover by RYAN JAMPOLE
Editorial supervision by ALESSANDRA BERELLO and LISA CAPIOTTO
(Atlantyca S.p.A.)
Script by CORTNEY POWELL
Art by RYAN JAMPOLE
Color by LAURIE E. SMITH
Lettering by WILSON RAMOS JR.

Production – JAYJAY JACKSON
Assistant Managing Editor – JEFF WHITMAN
JIM SALICRUP
Editor-in-Chief

ISBN 978-1-5458-0157-4

Printed in China
October 2018

Papercutz books may be purchased for business or promotional use.
For information on bulk purchases, please contact Macmillan
Corporate and Premium Sales Department at (800) 221-7945 x5442.

Distributed by Macmillan
First Printing

THE FASHION CLUB OF COLORS

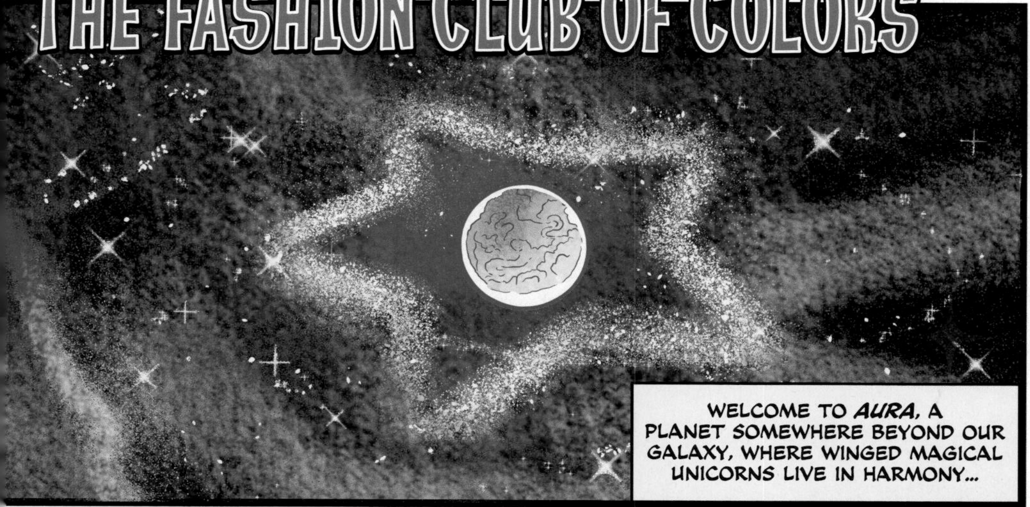
WELCOME TO AURA, A PLANET SOMEWHERE BEYOND OUR GALAXY, WHERE WINGED MAGICAL UNICORNS LIVE IN HARMONY...

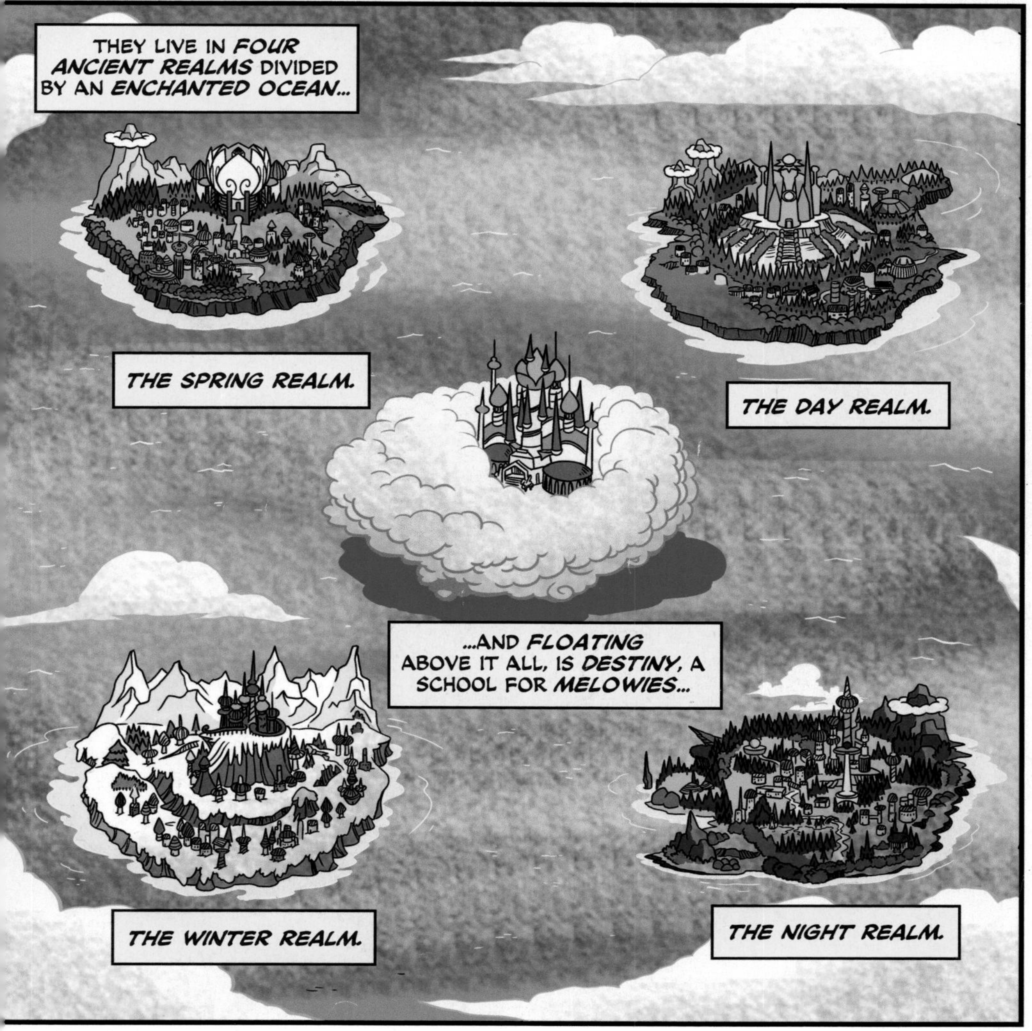
THEY LIVE IN FOUR ANCIENT REALMS DIVIDED BY AN ENCHANTED OCEAN...
THE SPRING REALM.
THE DAY REALM.
...AND FLOATING ABOVE IT ALL, IS DESTINY, A SCHOOL FOR MELOWIES...
THE WINTER REALM.
THE NIGHT REALM.

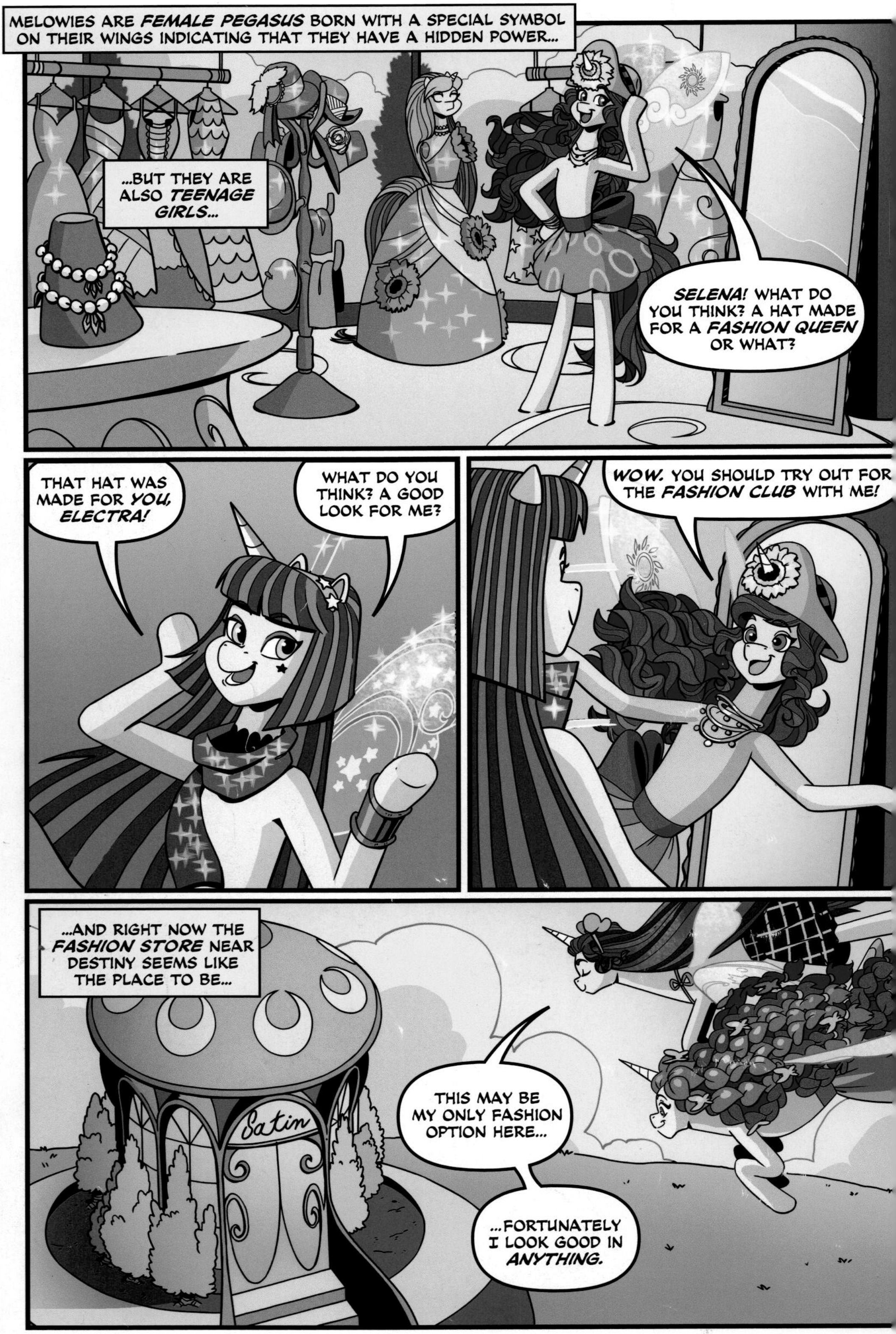
MELOWIES ARE FEMALE PEGASUS BORN WITH A SPECIAL SYMBOL ON THEIR WINGS INDICATING THAT THEY HAVE A HIDDEN POWER...
...BUT THEY ARE ALSO TEENAGE GIRLS...
SELENA! WHAT DO YOU THINK? A HAT MADE FOR A FASHION QUEEN OR WHAT?
THAT HAT WAS MADE FOR YOU, ELECTRA!
WHAT DO YOU THINK? A GOOD LOOK FOR ME?
WOW. YOU SHOULD TRY OUT FOR THE FASHION CLUB WITH ME!
...AND RIGHT NOW THE FASHION STORE NEAR DESTINY SEEMS LIKE THE PLACE TO BE...
Satin
THIS MAY BE MY ONLY FASHION OPTION HERE...
...FORTUNATELY I LOOK GOOD IN ANYTHING.

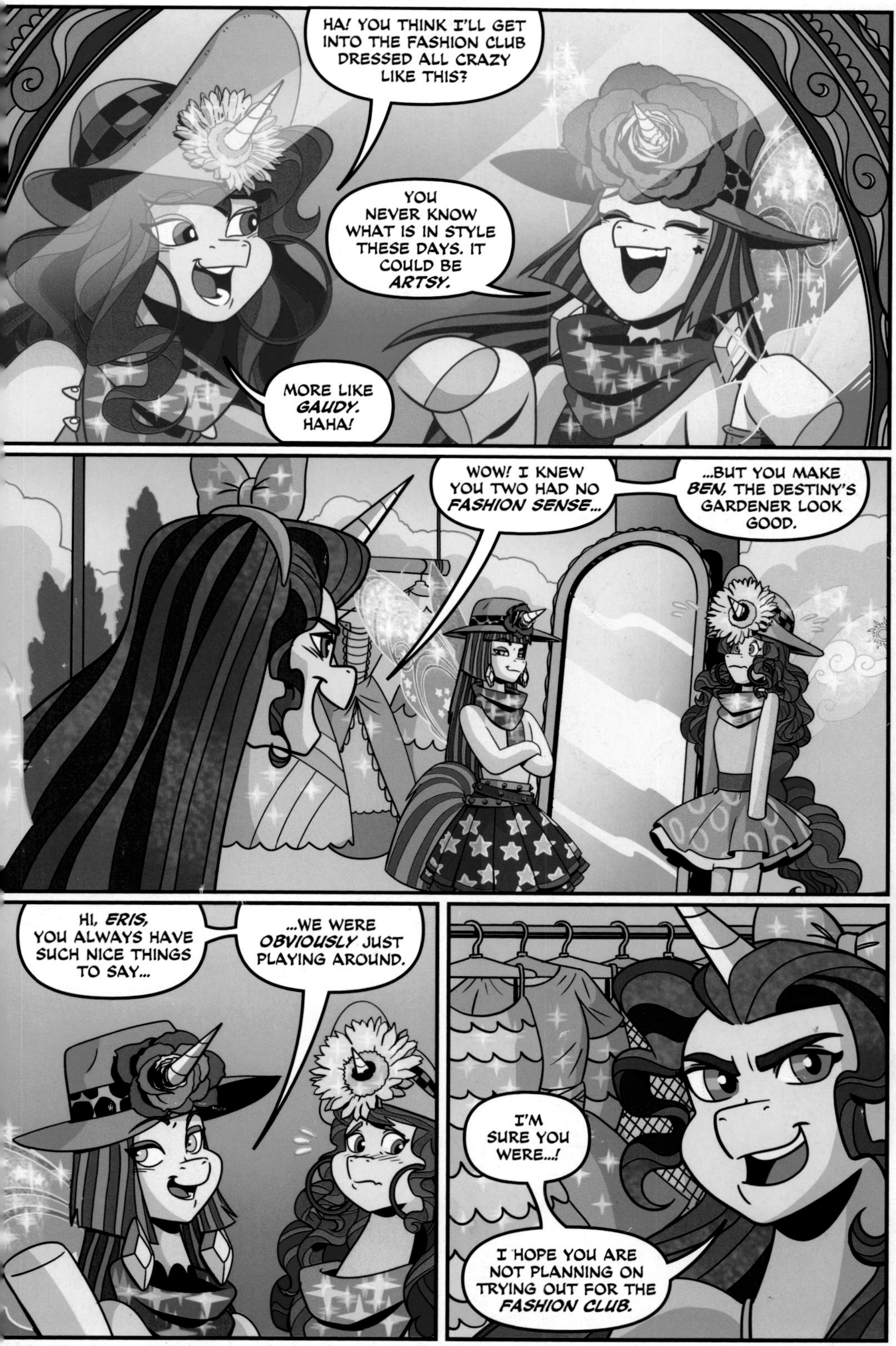
HA! YOU THINK I'LL GET INTO THE FASHION CLUB DRESSED ALL CRAZY LIKE THIS?
YOU NEVER KNOW WHAT IS IN STYLE THESE DAYS. IT COULD BE *ARTSY.*
MORE LIKE *GAUDY.* HAHA!
WOW! I KNEW YOU TWO HAD NO *FASHION SENSE*...
...BUT YOU MAKE *BEN,* THE DESTINY'S GARDENER LOOK GOOD.
HI, *ERIS,* YOU ALWAYS HAVE SUCH NICE THINGS TO SAY...
...WE WERE *OBVIOUSLY* JUST PLAYING AROUND.
I'M SURE YOU WERE...!
I HOPE YOU ARE NOT PLANNING ON TRYING OUT FOR THE *FASHION CLUB.*

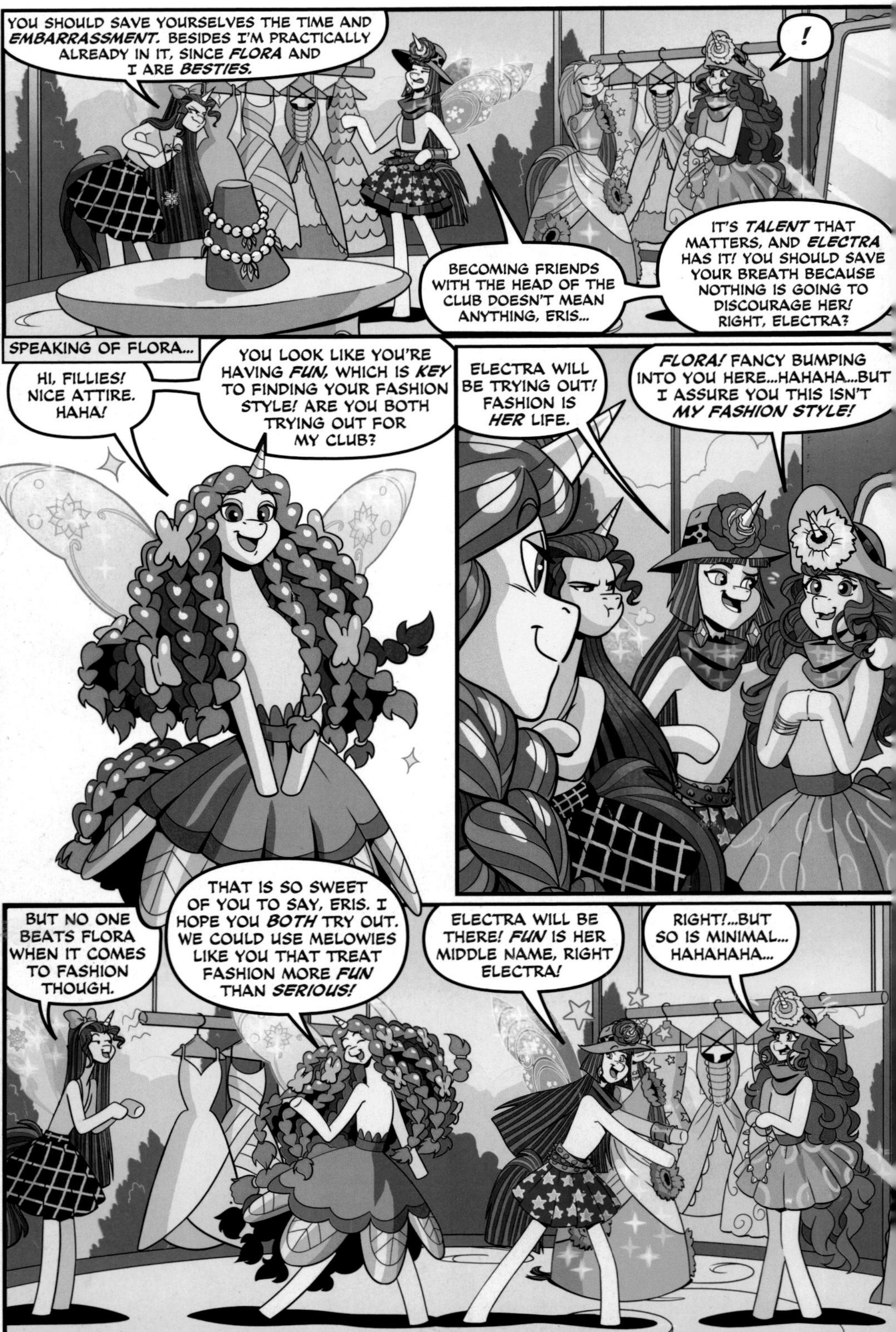
YOU SHOULD SAVE YOURSELVES THE TIME AND EMBARRASSMENT. BESIDES I'M PRACTICALLY ALREADY IN IT, SINCE FLORA AND I ARE BESTIES.
!
BECOMING FRIENDS WITH THE HEAD OF THE CLUB DOESN'T MEAN ANYTHING, ERIS...
IT'S TALENT THAT MATTERS, AND ELECTRA HAS IT! YOU SHOULD SAVE YOUR BREATH BECAUSE NOTHING IS GOING TO DISCOURAGE HER! RIGHT, ELECTRA?
SPEAKING OF FLORA...
HI, FILLIES! NICE ATTIRE. HAHA!
YOU LOOK LIKE YOU'RE HAVING FUN, WHICH IS KEY TO FINDING YOUR FASHION STYLE! ARE YOU BOTH TRYING OUT FOR MY CLUB?
ELECTRA WILL BE TRYING OUT! FASHION IS HER LIFE.
FLORA! FANCY BUMPING INTO YOU HERE...HAHAHA...BUT I ASSURE YOU THIS ISN'T MY FASHION STYLE!
BUT NO ONE BEATS FLORA WHEN IT COMES TO FASHION THOUGH.
THAT IS SO SWEET OF YOU TO SAY, ERIS. I HOPE YOU BOTH TRY OUT. WE COULD USE MELOWIES LIKE YOU THAT TREAT FASHION MORE FUN THAN SERIOUS!
ELECTRA WILL BE THERE! FUN IS HER MIDDLE NAME, RIGHT ELECTRA!
RIGHT!...BUT SO IS MINIMAL... HAHAHAHA...

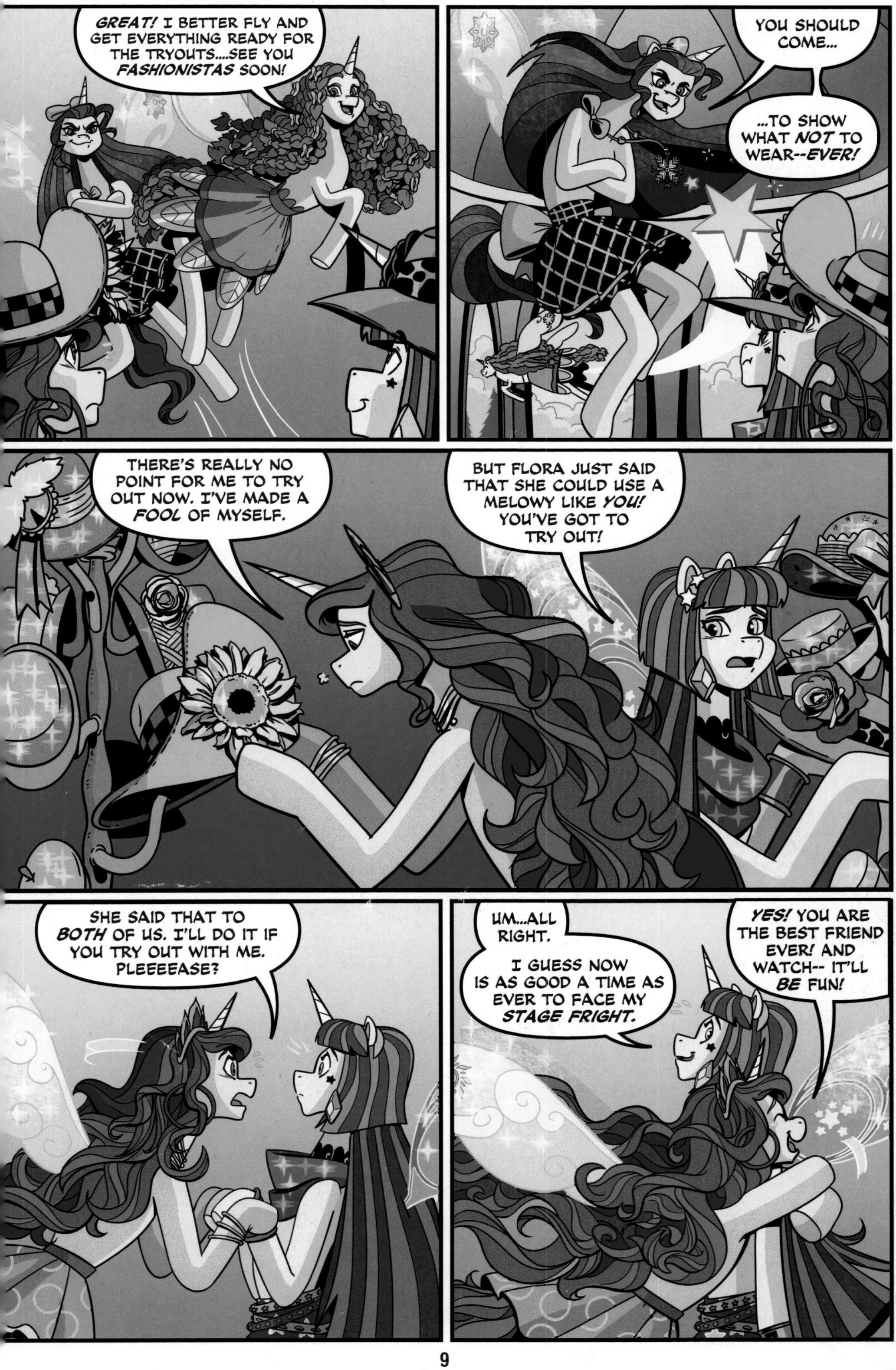
GREAT! I BETTER FLY AND GET EVERYTHING READY FOR THE TRYOUTS....SEE YOU FASHIONISTAS SOON!
YOU SHOULD COME...
...TO SHOW WHAT NOT TO WEAR--EVER!
THERE'S REALLY NO POINT FOR ME TO TRY OUT NOW. I'VE MADE A FOOL OF MYSELF.
BUT FLORA JUST SAID THAT SHE COULD USE A MELOWY LIKE YOU! YOU'VE GOT TO TRY OUT!
SHE SAID THAT TO BOTH OF US. I'LL DO IT IF YOU TRY OUT WITH ME. PLEEEEEASE?
UM...ALL RIGHT.
I GUESS NOW IS AS GOOD A TIME AS EVER TO FACE MY STAGE FRIGHT.
YES! YOU ARE THE BEST FRIEND EVER! AND WATCH-- IT'LL BE FUN!

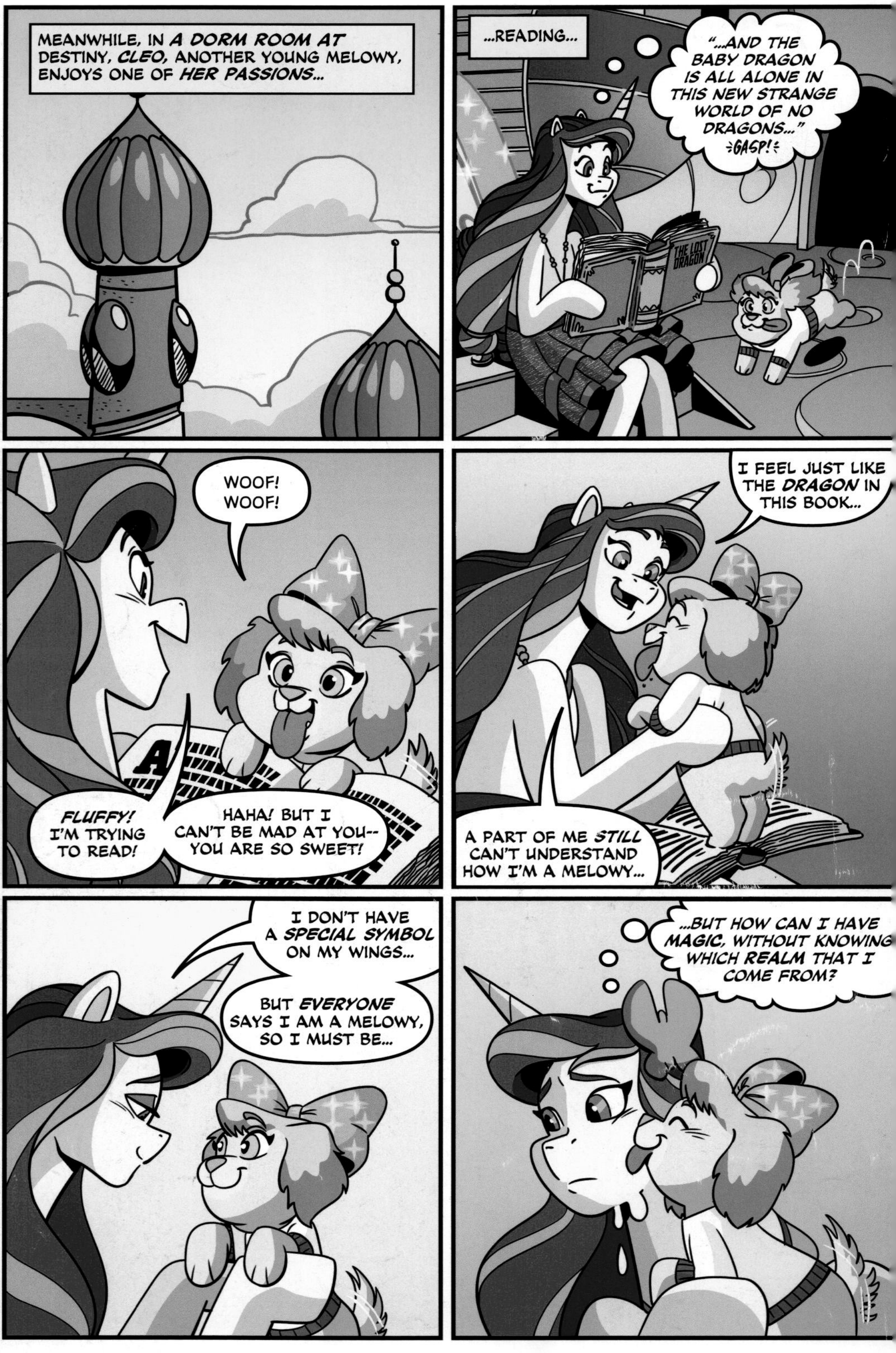

MEANWHILE, IN A DORM ROOM AT DESTINY, CLEO, ANOTHER YOUNG MELOWY, ENJOYS ONE OF HER PASSIONS...
...READING...
"...AND THE BABY DRAGON IS ALL ALONE IN THIS NEW STRANGE WORLD OF NO DRAGONS..." GASP!
THE LOST DRAGON
WOOF! WOOF!
FLUFFY! I'M TRYING TO READ!
HAHA! BUT I CAN'T BE MAD AT YOU-- YOU ARE SO SWEET!
I FEEL JUST LIKE THE DRAGON IN THIS BOOK...
A PART OF ME STILL CAN'T UNDERSTAND HOW I'M A MELOWY...
I DON'T HAVE A SPECIAL SYMBOL ON MY WINGS...
BUT EVERYONE SAYS I AM A MELOWY, SO I MUST BE...
...BUT HOW CAN I HAVE MAGIC, WITHOUT KNOWING WHICH REALM THAT I COME FROM?

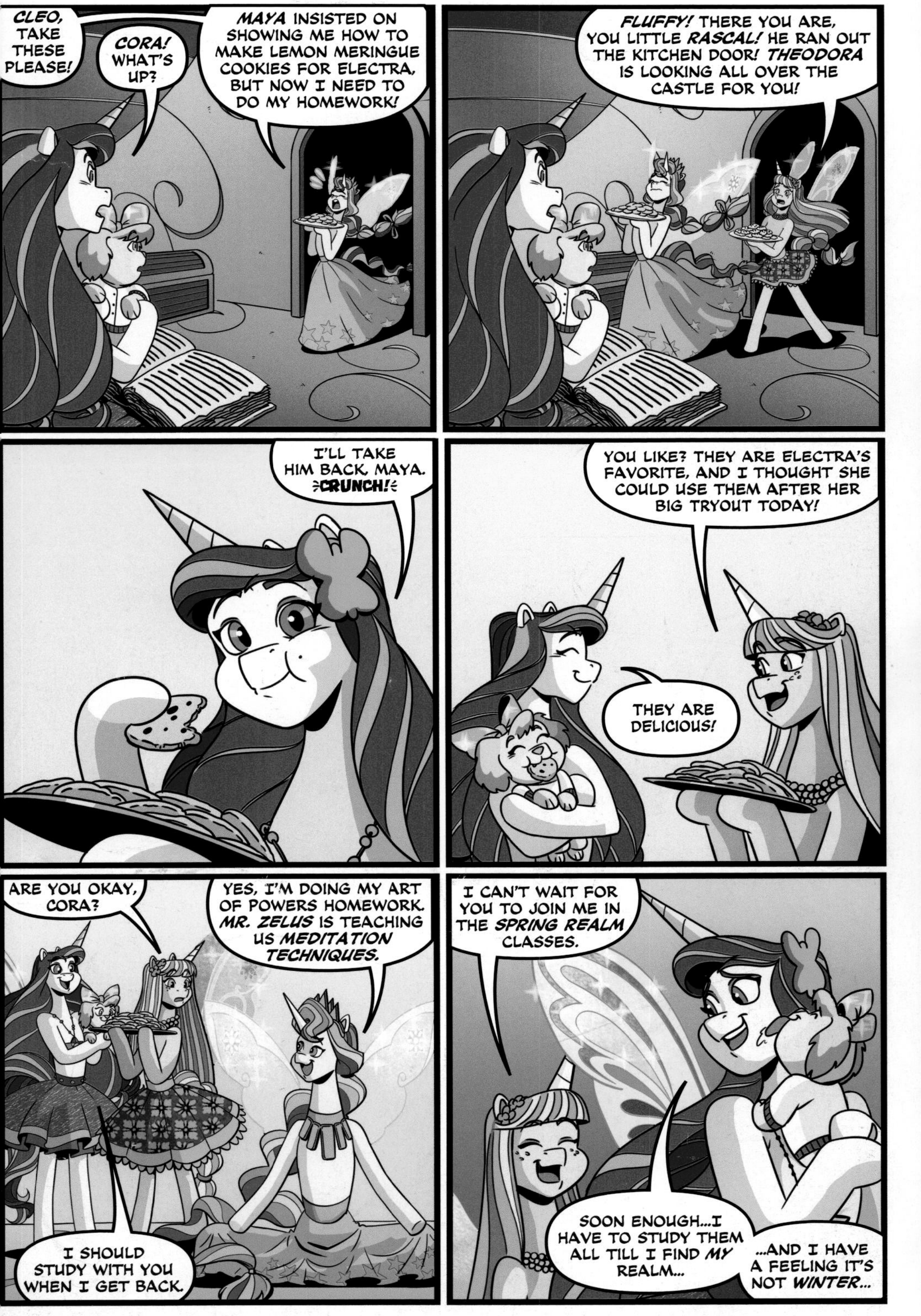
CLEO, TAKE THESE PLEASE!
CORA! WHAT'S UP?
MAYA INSISTED ON SHOWING ME HOW TO MAKE LEMON MERINGUE COOKIES FOR ELECTRA, BUT NOW I NEED TO DO MY HOMEWORK!
FLUFFY! THERE YOU ARE, YOU LITTLE RASCAL! HE RAN OUT THE KITCHEN DOOR! THEODORA IS LOOKING ALL OVER THE CASTLE FOR YOU!
I'LL TAKE HIM BACK, MAYA.
CRUNCH!
YOU LIKE? THEY ARE ELECTRA'S FAVORITE, AND I THOUGHT SHE COULD USE THEM AFTER HER BIG TRYOUT TODAY!
THEY ARE DELICIOUS!
ARE YOU OKAY, CORA?
YES, I'M DOING MY ART OF POWERS HOMEWORK. MR. ZELUS IS TEACHING US MEDITATION TECHNIQUES.
I SHOULD STUDY WITH YOU WHEN I GET BACK.
I CAN'T WAIT FOR YOU TO JOIN ME IN THE SPRING REALM CLASSES.
SOON ENOUGH...I HAVE TO STUDY THEM ALL TILL I FIND MY REALM...
...AND I HAVE A FEELING IT'S NOT WINTER...

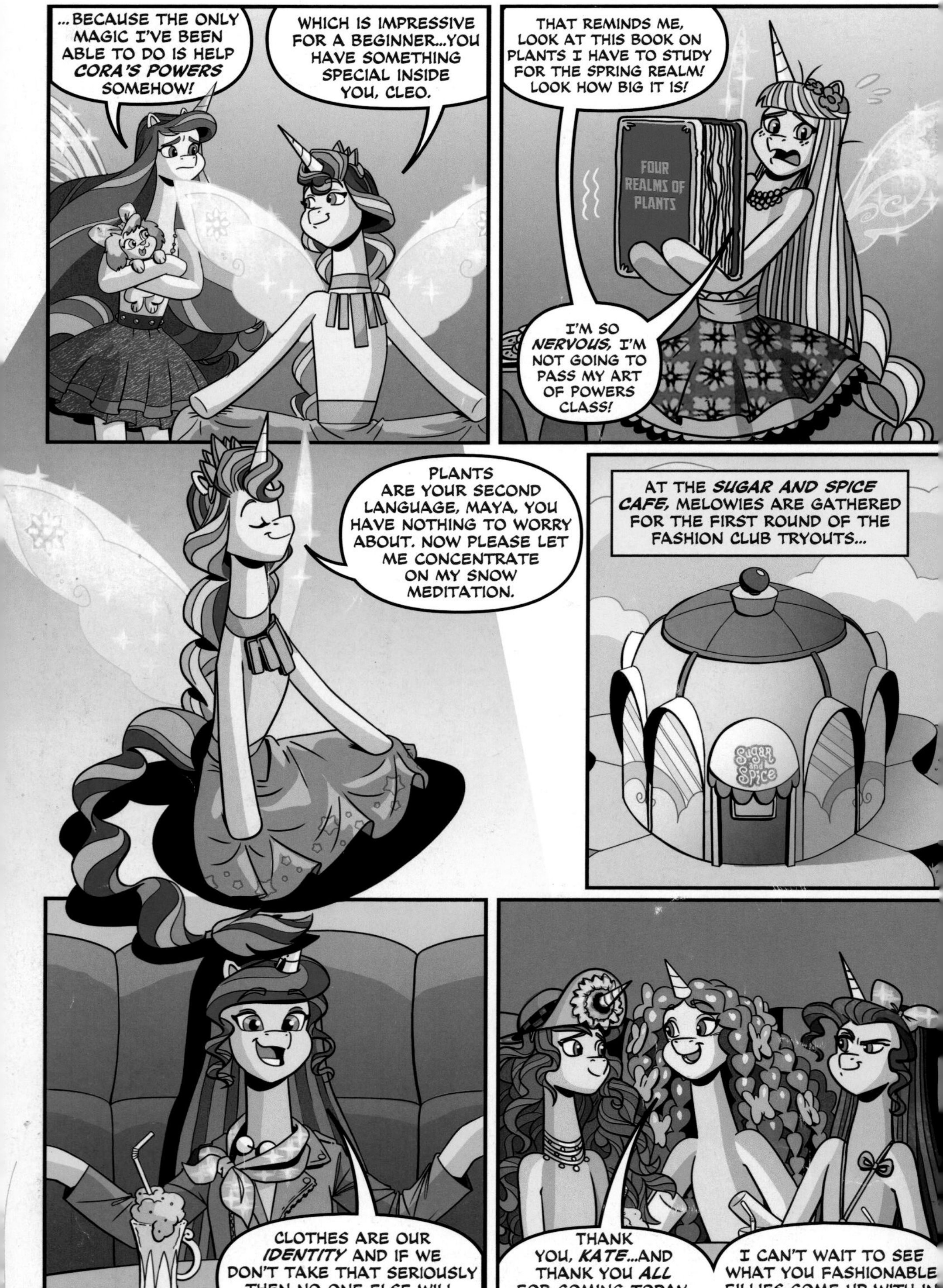
...BECAUSE THE ONLY MAGIC I'VE BEEN ABLE TO DO IS HELP CORA'S POWERS SOMEHOW!
WHICH IS IMPRESSIVE FOR A BEGINNER...YOU HAVE SOMETHING SPECIAL INSIDE YOU, CLEO.
THAT REMINDS ME, LOOK AT THIS BOOK ON PLANTS I HAVE TO STUDY FOR THE SPRING REALM! LOOK HOW BIG IT IS!
FOUR REALMS OF PLANTS
I'M SO NERVOUS, I'M NOT GOING TO PASS MY ART OF POWERS CLASS!
PLANTS ARE YOUR SECOND LANGUAGE, MAYA, YOU HAVE NOTHING TO WORRY ABOUT. NOW PLEASE LET ME CONCENTRATE ON MY SNOW MEDITATION.
AT THE SUGAR AND SPICE CAFE, MELOWIES ARE GATHERED FOR THE FIRST ROUND OF THE FASHION CLUB TRYOUTS...
Sugar and Spice
CLOTHES ARE OUR IDENTITY AND IF WE DON'T TAKE THAT SERIOUSLY THEN NO ONE ELSE WILL. THAT'S WHAT FASHION MEANS TO ME.
THANK YOU, KATE...AND THANK YOU ALL FOR COMING TODAY. YOUR ENERGIES HAVE BEEN INSPIRING.
I CAN'T WAIT TO SEE WHAT YOU FASHIONABLE FILLIES COME UP WITH IN THE SECOND AND FINAL ROUND OF TRYOUTS.

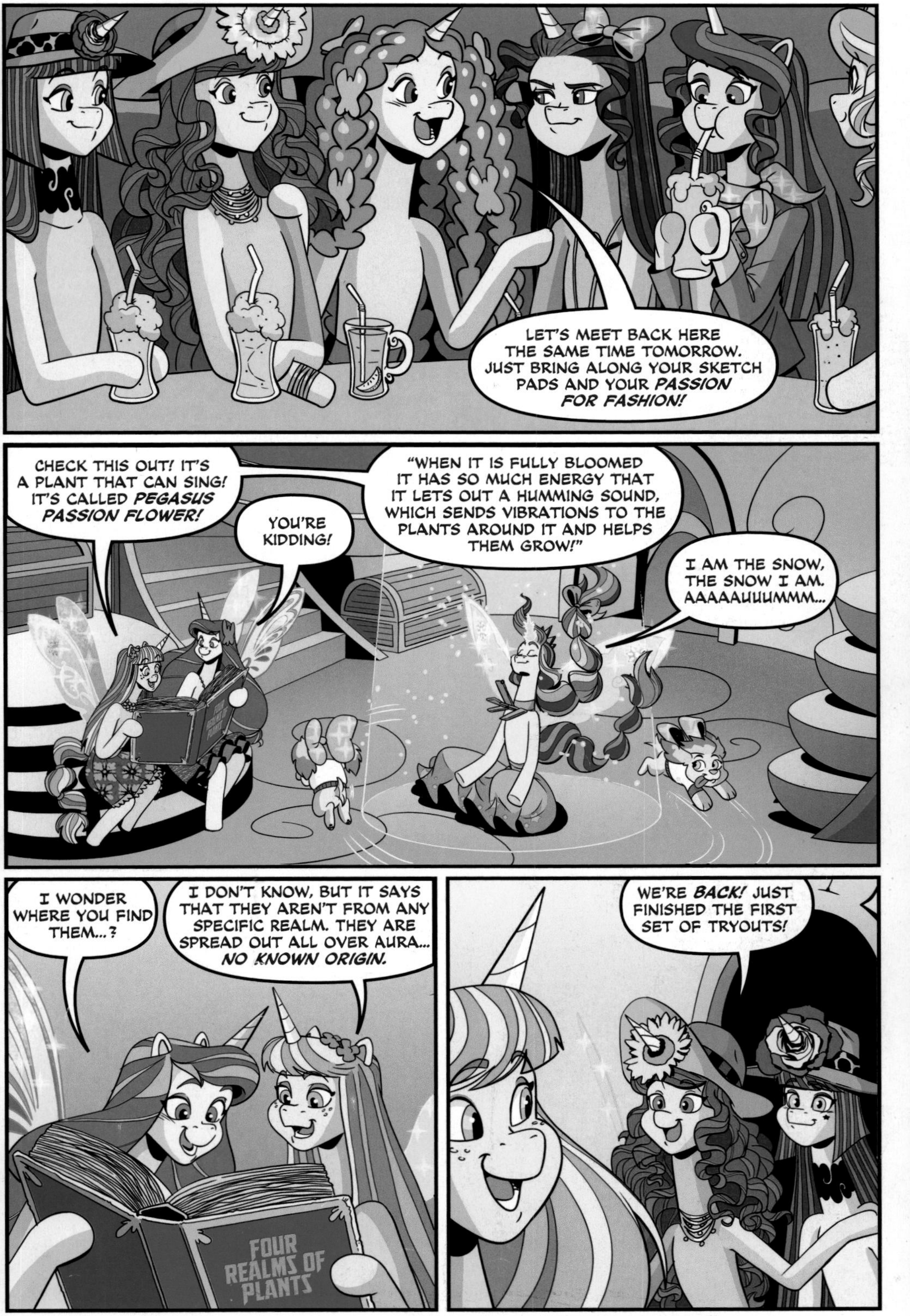
LET'S MEET BACK HERE THE SAME TIME TOMORROW. JUST BRING ALONG YOUR SKETCH PADS AND YOUR *PASSION FOR FASHION!*
CHECK THIS OUT! IT'S A PLANT THAT CAN SING! IT'S CALLED *PEGASUS PASSION FLOWER!*
YOU'RE KIDDING!
"WHEN IT IS FULLY BLOOMED IT HAS SO MUCH ENERGY THAT IT LETS OUT A HUMMING SOUND, WHICH SENDS VIBRATIONS TO THE PLANTS AROUND IT AND HELPS THEM GROW!"
I AM THE SNOW, THE SNOW I AM. AAAAAUUUMMM...
FOUR REALMS OF PLANTS
I WONDER WHERE YOU FIND THEM...?
I DON'T KNOW, BUT IT SAYS THAT THEY AREN'T FROM ANY SPECIFIC REALM. THEY ARE SPREAD OUT ALL OVER AURA... *NO KNOWN ORIGIN.*
FOUR REALMS OF PLANTS
WE'RE *BACK!* JUST FINISHED THE FIRST SET OF TRYOUTS!

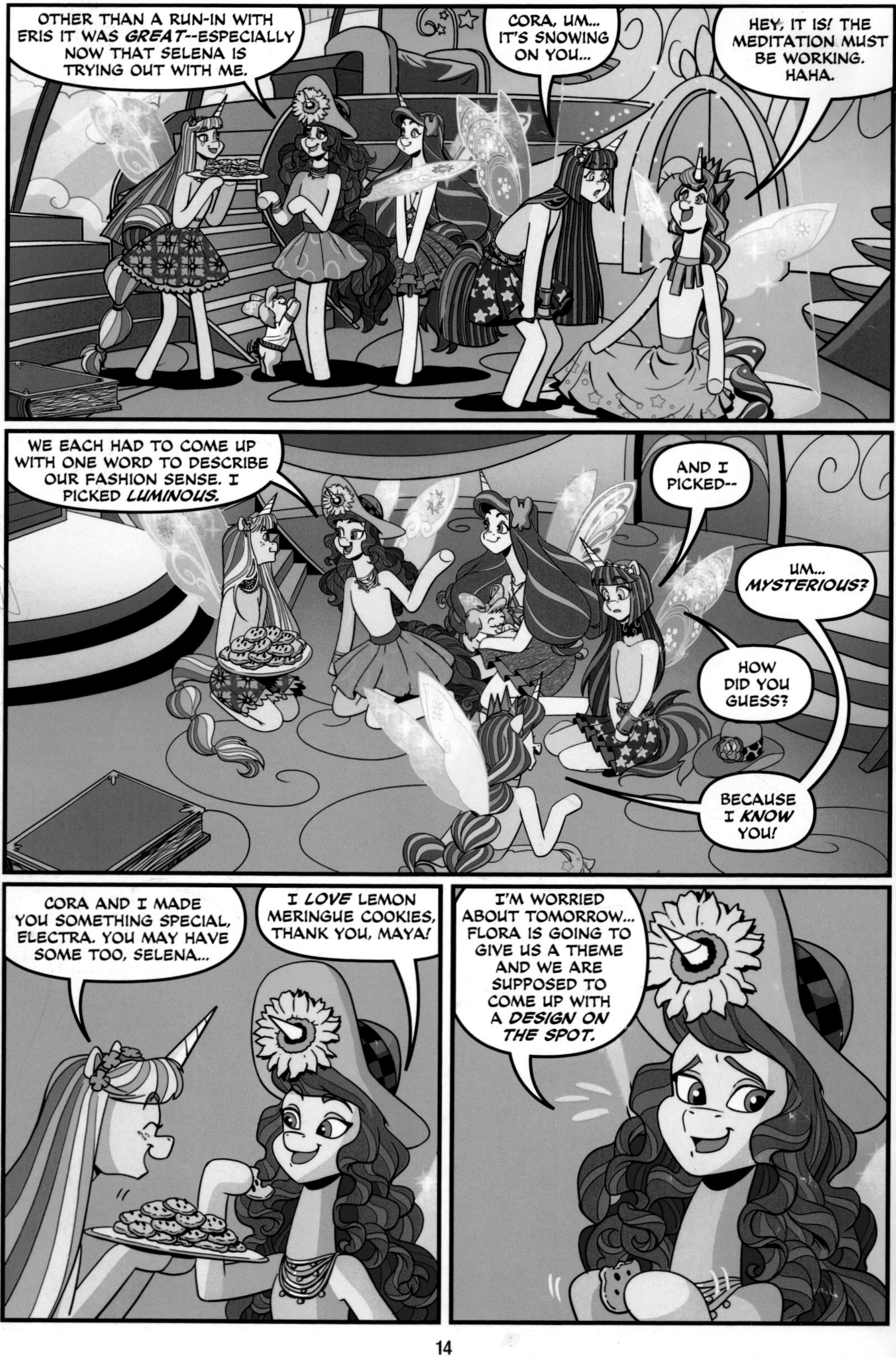
OTHER THAN A RUN-IN WITH ERIS IT WAS GREAT--ESPECIALLY NOW THAT SELENA IS TRYING OUT WITH ME.
CORA, UM... IT'S SNOWING ON YOU...
HEY, IT IS! THE MEDITATION MUST BE WORKING. HAHA.
WE EACH HAD TO COME UP WITH ONE WORD TO DESCRIBE OUR FASHION SENSE. I PICKED LUMINOUS.
AND I PICKED--
UM... MYSTERIOUS?
HOW DID YOU GUESS?
BECAUSE I KNOW YOU!
CORA AND I MADE YOU SOMETHING SPECIAL, ELECTRA. YOU MAY HAVE SOME TOO, SELENA...
I LOVE LEMON MERINGUE COOKIES, THANK YOU, MAYA!
I'M WORRIED ABOUT TOMORROW... FLORA IS GOING TO GIVE US A THEME AND WE ARE SUPPOSED TO COME UP WITH A DESIGN ON THE SPOT.

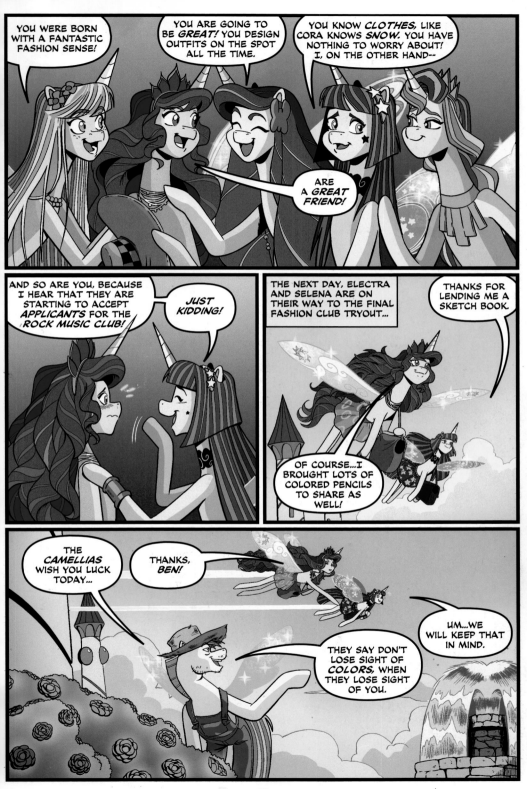

YOU WERE BORN WITH A FANTASTIC FASHION SENSE!

YOU ARE GOING TO BE *GREAT!* YOU DESIGN OUTFITS ON THE SPOT ALL THE TIME.

YOU KNOW *CLOTHES*, LIKE CORA KNOWS *SNOW*. YOU HAVE NOTHING TO WORRY ABOUT! I, ON THE OTHER HAND--

ARE A *GREAT FRIEND!*

AND SO ARE YOU, BECAUSE I HEAR THAT THEY ARE STARTING TO ACCEPT *APPLICANTS* FOR THE *ROCK MUSIC CLUB!*

JUST KIDDING!

THE NEXT DAY, ELECTRA AND SELENA ARE ON THEIR WAY TO THE FINAL FASHION CLUB TRYOUT...

THANKS FOR LENDING ME A SKETCH BOOK.

OF COURSE...I BROUGHT LOTS OF COLORED PENCILS TO SHARE AS WELL!

THE *CAMELLIAS* WISH YOU LUCK TODAY...

THANKS, *BEN!*

THEY SAY DON'T LOSE SIGHT OF *COLORS*, WHEN THEY LOSE SIGHT OF YOU.

UM...WE WILL KEEP THAT IN MIND.

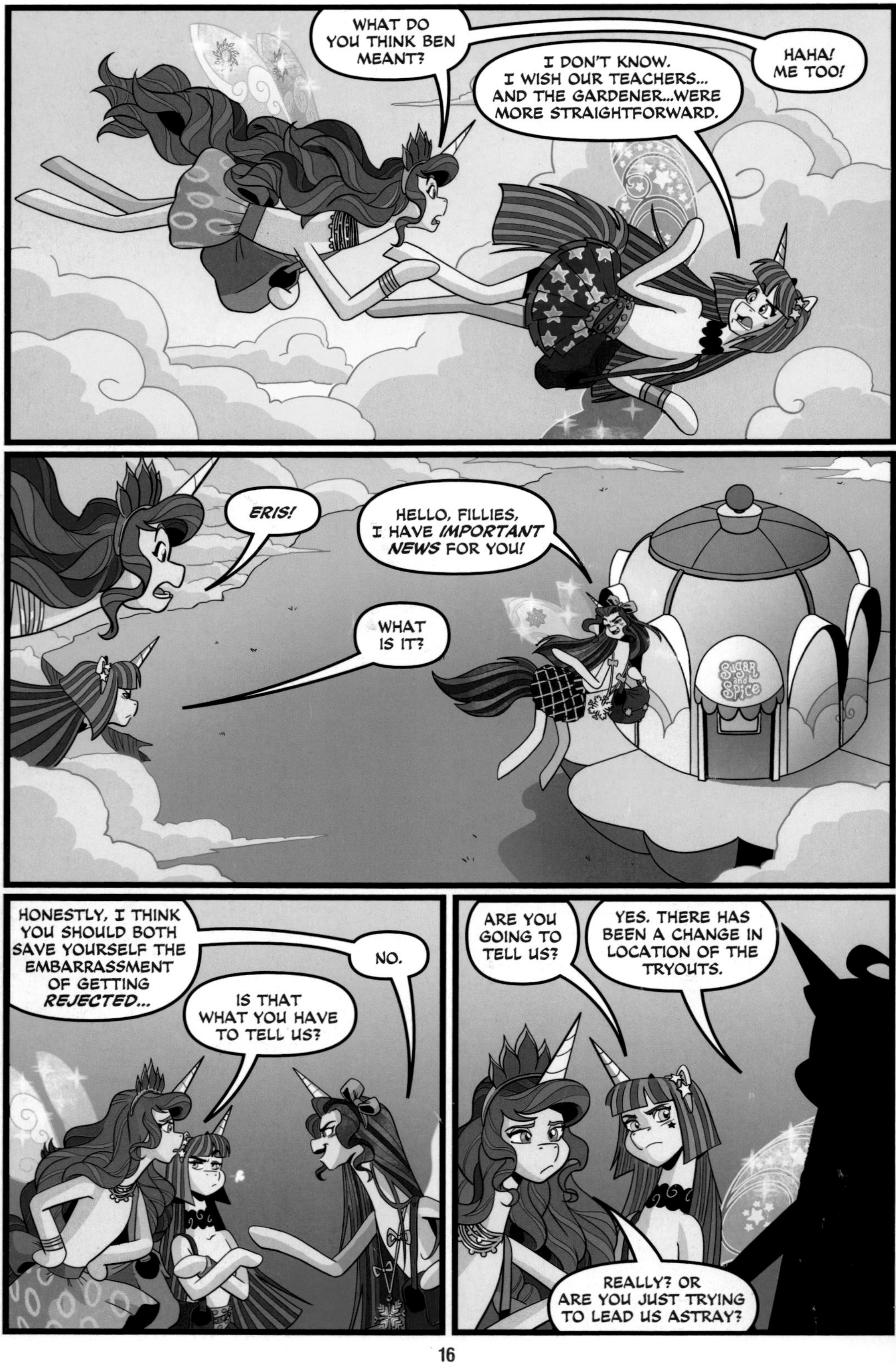
WHAT DO YOU THINK BEN MEANT?
I DON'T KNOW. I WISH OUR TEACHERS... AND THE GARDENER...WERE MORE STRAIGHTFORWARD.
HAHA! ME TOO!
ERIS!
HELLO, FILLIES, I HAVE IMPORTANT NEWS FOR YOU!
WHAT IS IT?
Sugar and Spice
HONESTLY, I THINK YOU SHOULD BOTH SAVE YOURSELF THE EMBARRASSMENT OF GETTING REJECTED...
NO.
IS THAT WHAT YOU HAVE TO TELL US?
ARE YOU GOING TO TELL US?
YES. THERE HAS BEEN A CHANGE IN LOCATION OF THE TRYOUTS.
REALLY? OR ARE YOU JUST TRYING TO LEAD US ASTRAY?

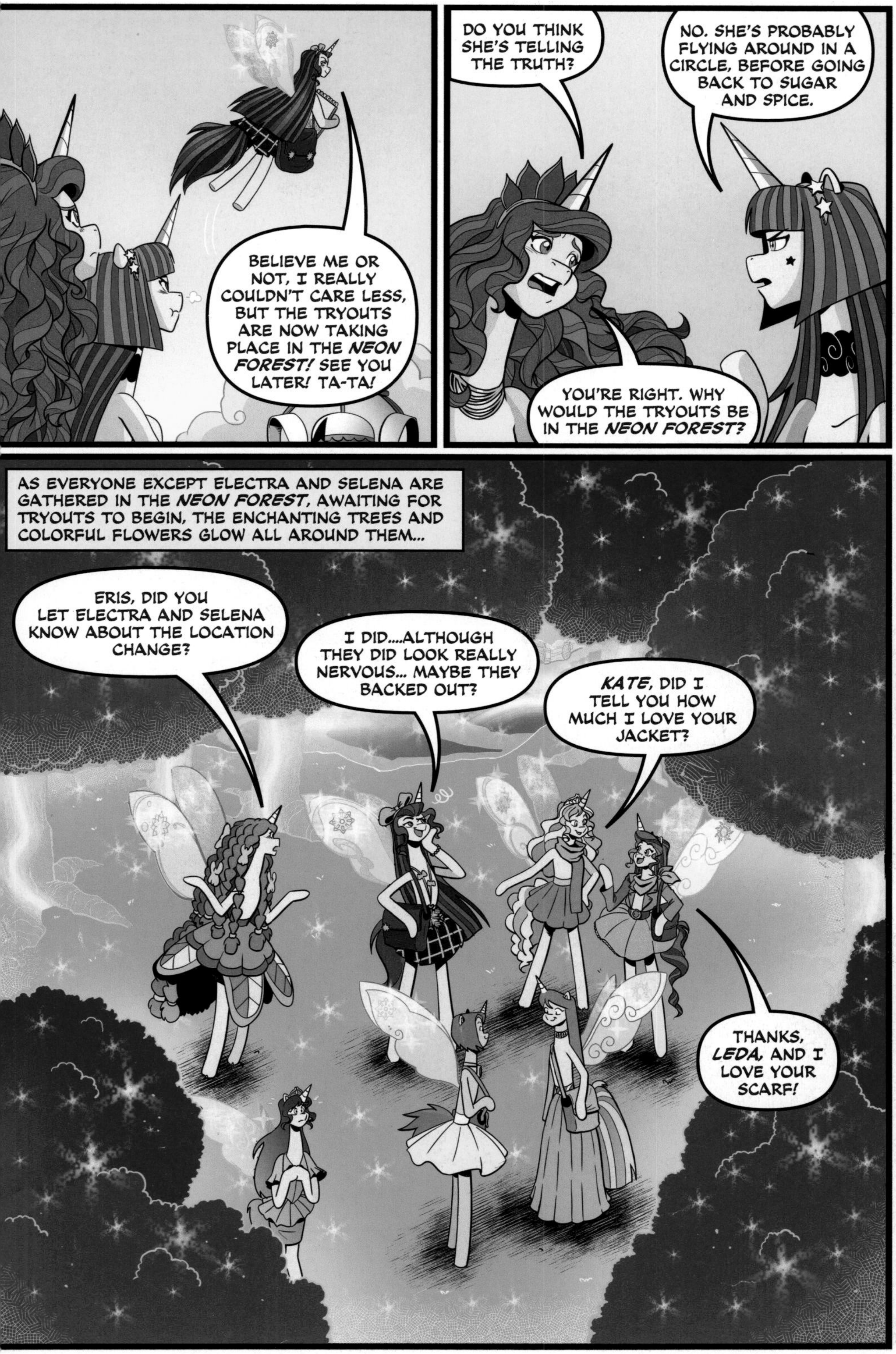
BELIEVE ME OR NOT, I REALLY COULDN'T CARE LESS, BUT THE TRYOUTS ARE NOW TAKING PLACE IN THE *NEON FOREST!* SEE YOU LATER! TA-TA!
DO YOU THINK SHE'S TELLING THE TRUTH?
NO. SHE'S PROBABLY FLYING AROUND IN A CIRCLE, BEFORE GOING BACK TO SUGAR AND SPICE.
YOU'RE RIGHT. WHY WOULD THE TRYOUTS BE IN THE *NEON FOREST?*
AS EVERYONE EXCEPT ELECTRA AND SELENA ARE GATHERED IN THE *NEON FOREST*, AWAITING FOR TRYOUTS TO BEGIN, THE ENCHANTING TREES AND COLORFUL FLOWERS GLOW ALL AROUND THEM...
ERIS, DID YOU LET ELECTRA AND SELENA KNOW ABOUT THE LOCATION CHANGE?
I DID....ALTHOUGH THEY DID LOOK REALLY NERVOUS... MAYBE THEY BACKED OUT?
KATE, DID I TELL YOU HOW MUCH I LOVE YOUR JACKET?
THANKS, *LEDA*, AND I LOVE YOUR SCARF!

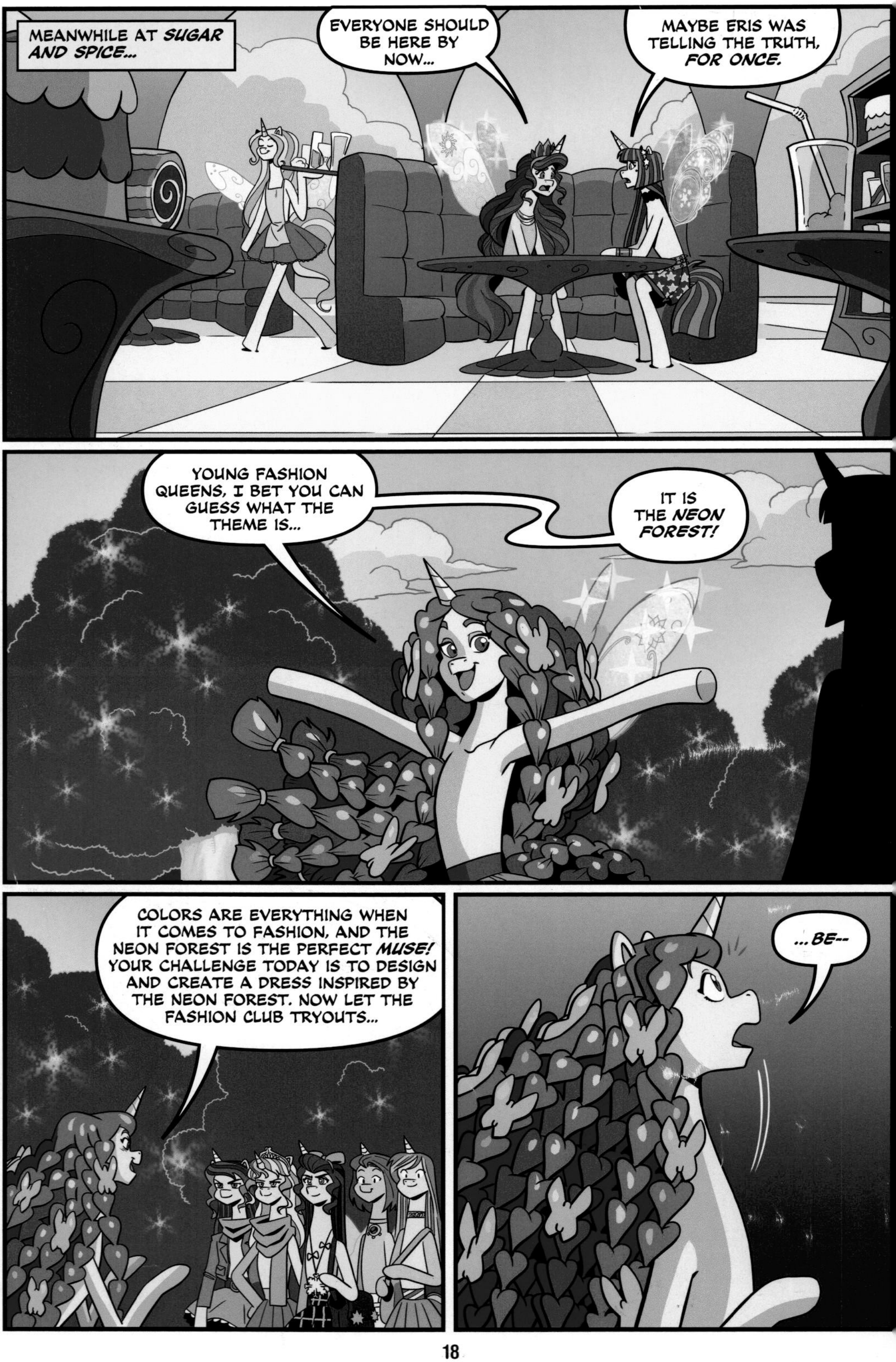
MEANWHILE AT *SUGAR AND SPICE...*
EVERYONE SHOULD BE HERE BY NOW...
MAYBE ERIS WAS TELLING THE TRUTH, *FOR ONCE.*
YOUNG FASHION QUEENS, I BET YOU CAN GUESS WHAT THE THEME IS...
IT IS THE *NEON FOREST!*
COLORS ARE EVERYTHING WHEN IT COMES TO FASHION, AND THE NEON FOREST IS THE PERFECT *MUSE!* YOUR CHALLENGE TODAY IS TO DESIGN AND CREATE A DRESS INSPIRED BY THE NEON FOREST. NOW LET THE FASHION CLUB TRYOUTS...
...BE--

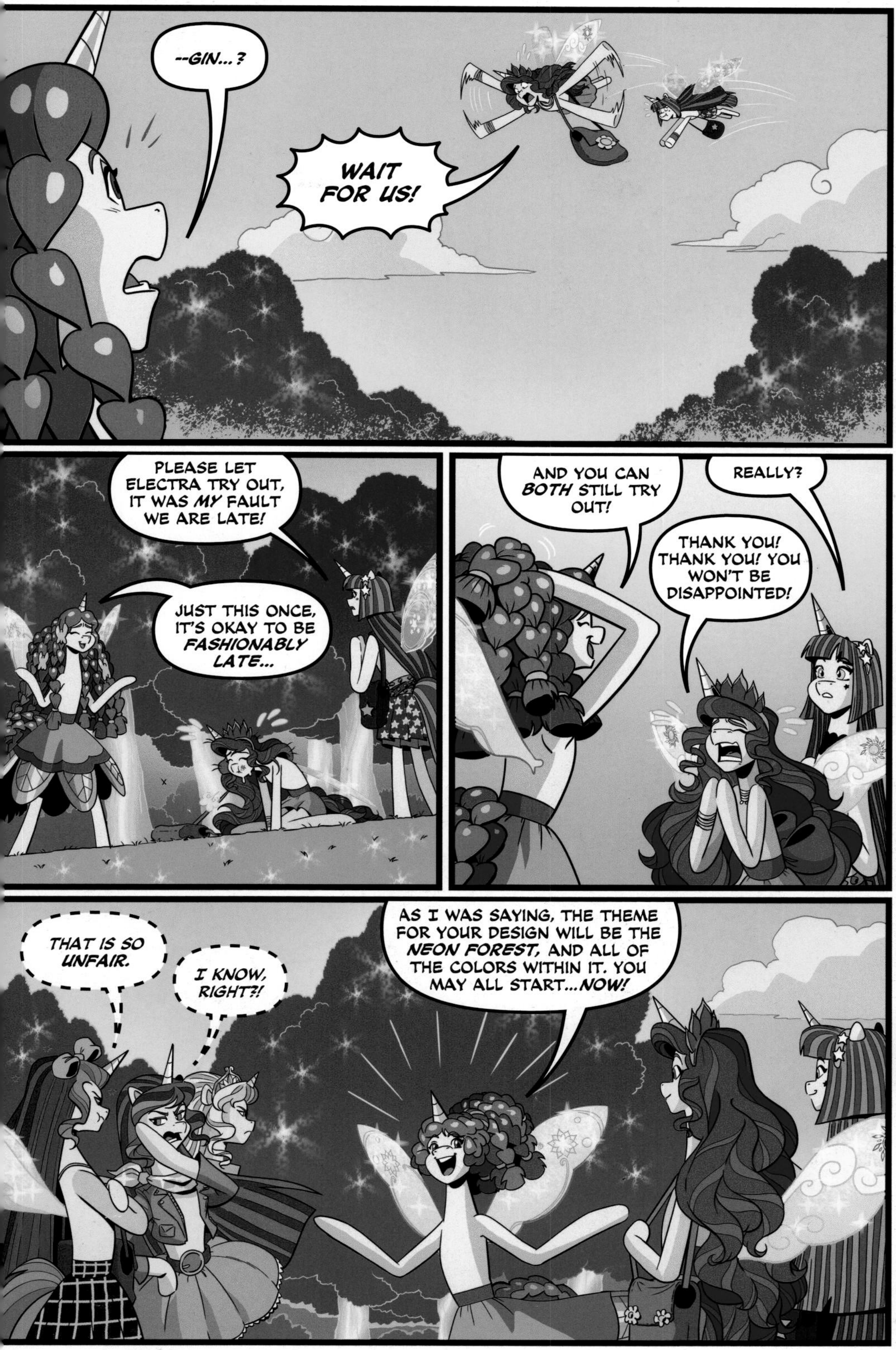
--GIN...?
WAIT FOR US!
PLEASE LET ELECTRA TRY OUT, IT WAS MY FAULT WE ARE LATE!
JUST THIS ONCE, IT'S OKAY TO BE FASHIONABLY LATE...
AND YOU CAN BOTH STILL TRY OUT!
REALLY?
THANK YOU! THANK YOU! YOU WON'T BE DISAPPOINTED!
THAT IS SO UNFAIR.
I KNOW, RIGHT?!
AS I WAS SAYING, THE THEME FOR YOUR DESIGN WILL BE THE NEON FOREST, AND ALL OF THE COLORS WITHIN IT. YOU MAY ALL START...NOW!

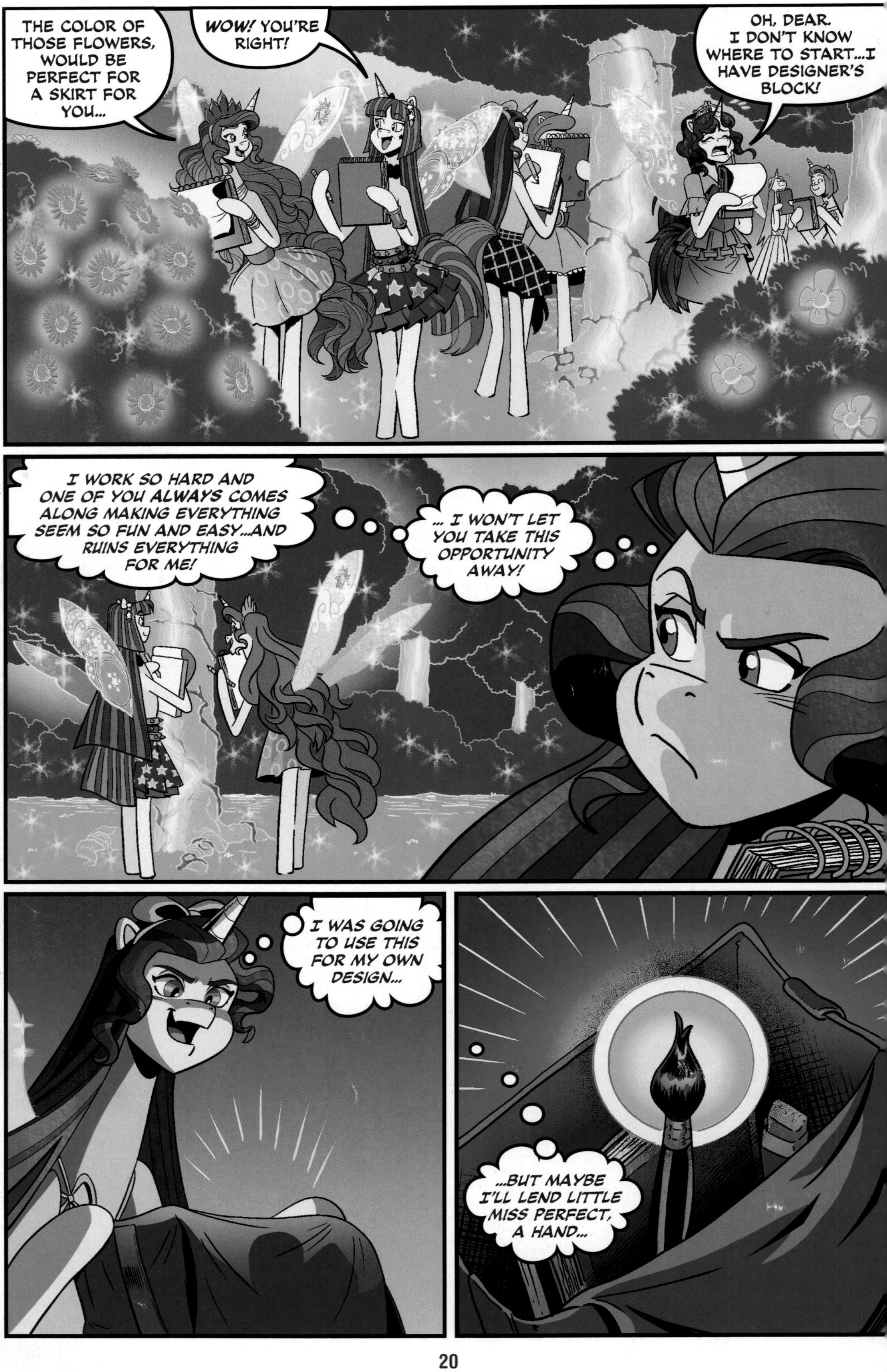
THE COLOR OF THOSE FLOWERS, WOULD BE PERFECT FOR A SKIRT FOR YOU...
WOW! YOU'RE RIGHT!
OH, DEAR. I DON'T KNOW WHERE TO START...I HAVE DESIGNER'S BLOCK!
I WORK SO HARD AND ONE OF YOU ALWAYS COMES ALONG MAKING EVERYTHING SEEM SO FUN AND EASY...AND RUINS EVERYTHING FOR ME!
... I WON'T LET YOU TAKE THIS OPPORTUNITY AWAY!
I WAS GOING TO USE THIS FOR MY OWN DESIGN...
...BUT MAYBE I'LL LEND LITTLE MISS PERFECT, A HAND...

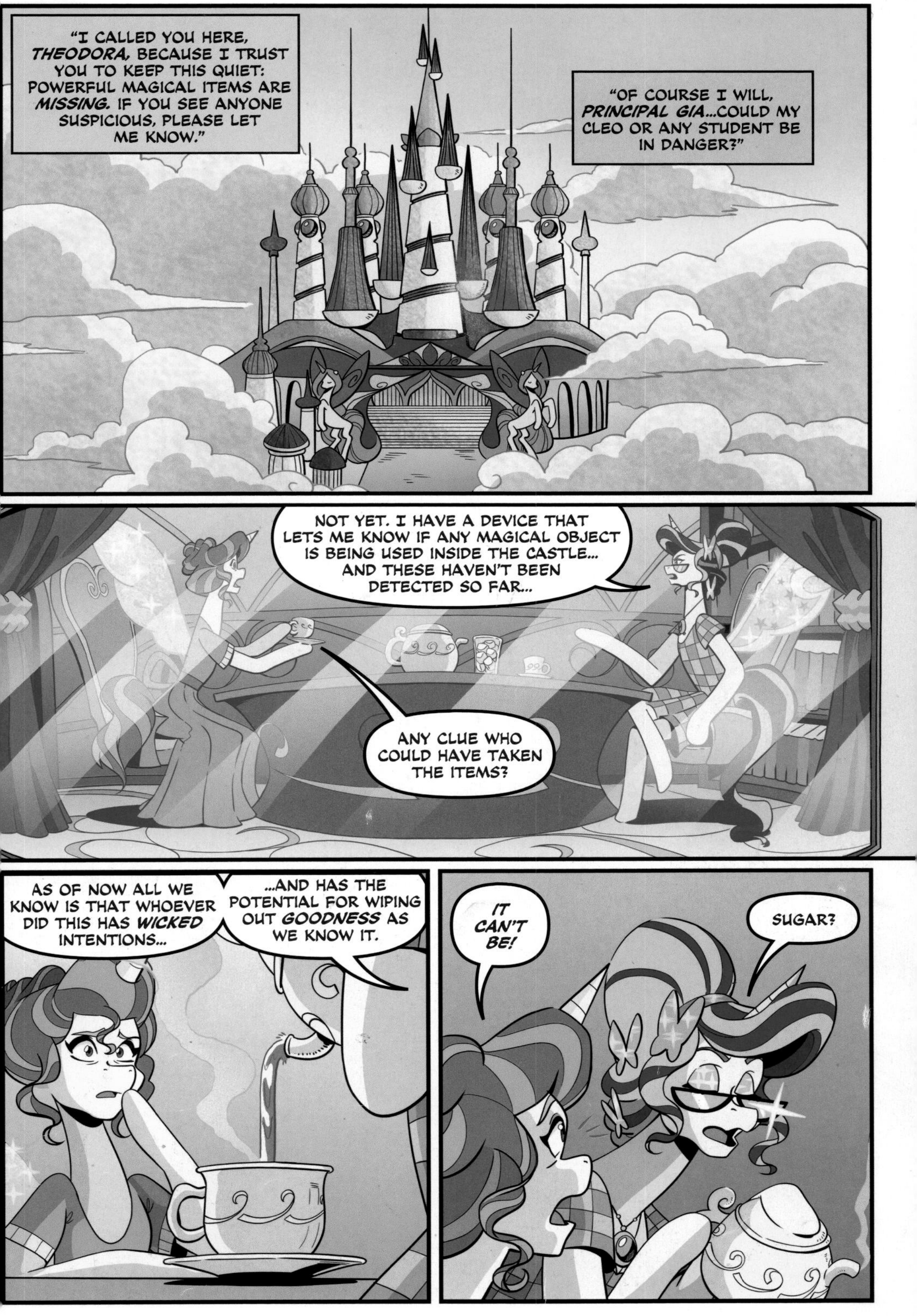
"I CALLED YOU HERE, *THEODORA,* BECAUSE I TRUST YOU TO KEEP THIS QUIET: POWERFUL MAGICAL ITEMS ARE *MISSING.* IF YOU SEE ANYONE SUSPICIOUS, PLEASE LET ME KNOW."
"OF COURSE I WILL, *PRINCIPAL GIA*...COULD MY CLEO OR ANY STUDENT BE IN DANGER?"
NOT YET. I HAVE A DEVICE THAT LETS ME KNOW IF ANY MAGICAL OBJECT IS BEING USED INSIDE THE CASTLE... AND THESE HAVEN'T BEEN DETECTED SO FAR...
ANY CLUE WHO COULD HAVE TAKEN THE ITEMS?
AS OF NOW ALL WE KNOW IS THAT WHOEVER DID THIS HAS *WICKED* INTENTIONS...
...AND HAS THE POTENTIAL FOR WIPING OUT *GOODNESS* AS WE KNOW IT.
IT CAN'T BE!
SUGAR?

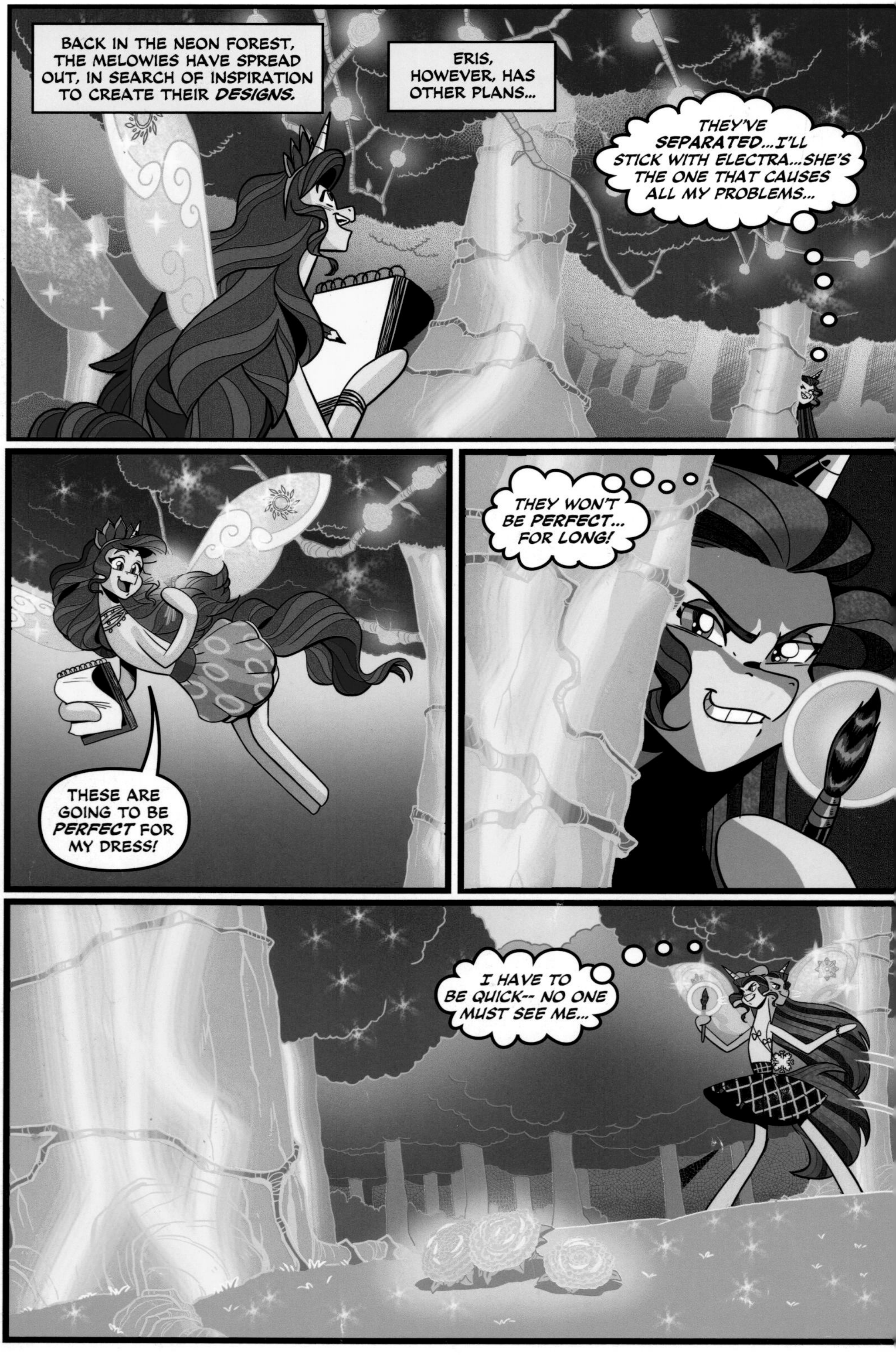
BACK IN THE NEON FOREST, THE MELOWIES HAVE SPREAD OUT, IN SEARCH OF INSPIRATION TO CREATE THEIR *DESIGNS.*
ERIS, HOWEVER, HAS OTHER PLANS...
THEY'VE *SEPARATED*...I'LL STICK WITH ELECTRA...SHE'S THE ONE THAT CAUSES ALL MY PROBLEMS...
THESE ARE GOING TO BE *PERFECT* FOR MY DRESS!
THEY WON'T BE *PERFECT*... FOR LONG!
I HAVE TO BE QUICK-- NO ONE MUST SEE ME...

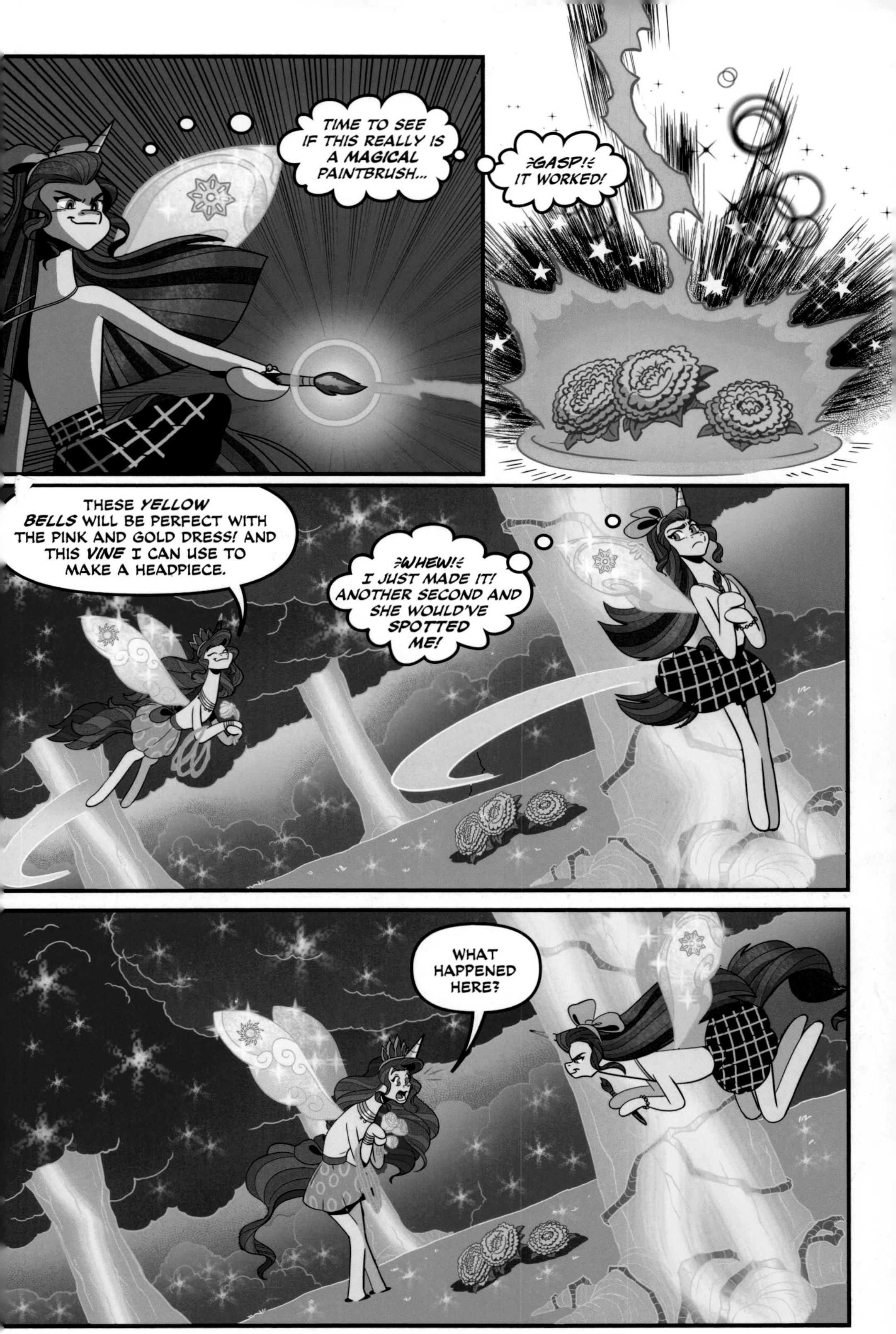
TIME TO SEE IF THIS REALLY IS A MAGICAL PAINTBRUSH...
GASP! IT WORKED!
THESE YELLOW BELLS WILL BE PERFECT WITH THE PINK AND GOLD DRESS! AND THIS VINE I CAN USE TO MAKE A HEADPIECE.
WHEW! I JUST MADE IT! ANOTHER SECOND AND SHE WOULD'VE SPOTTED ME!
WHAT HAPPENED HERE?

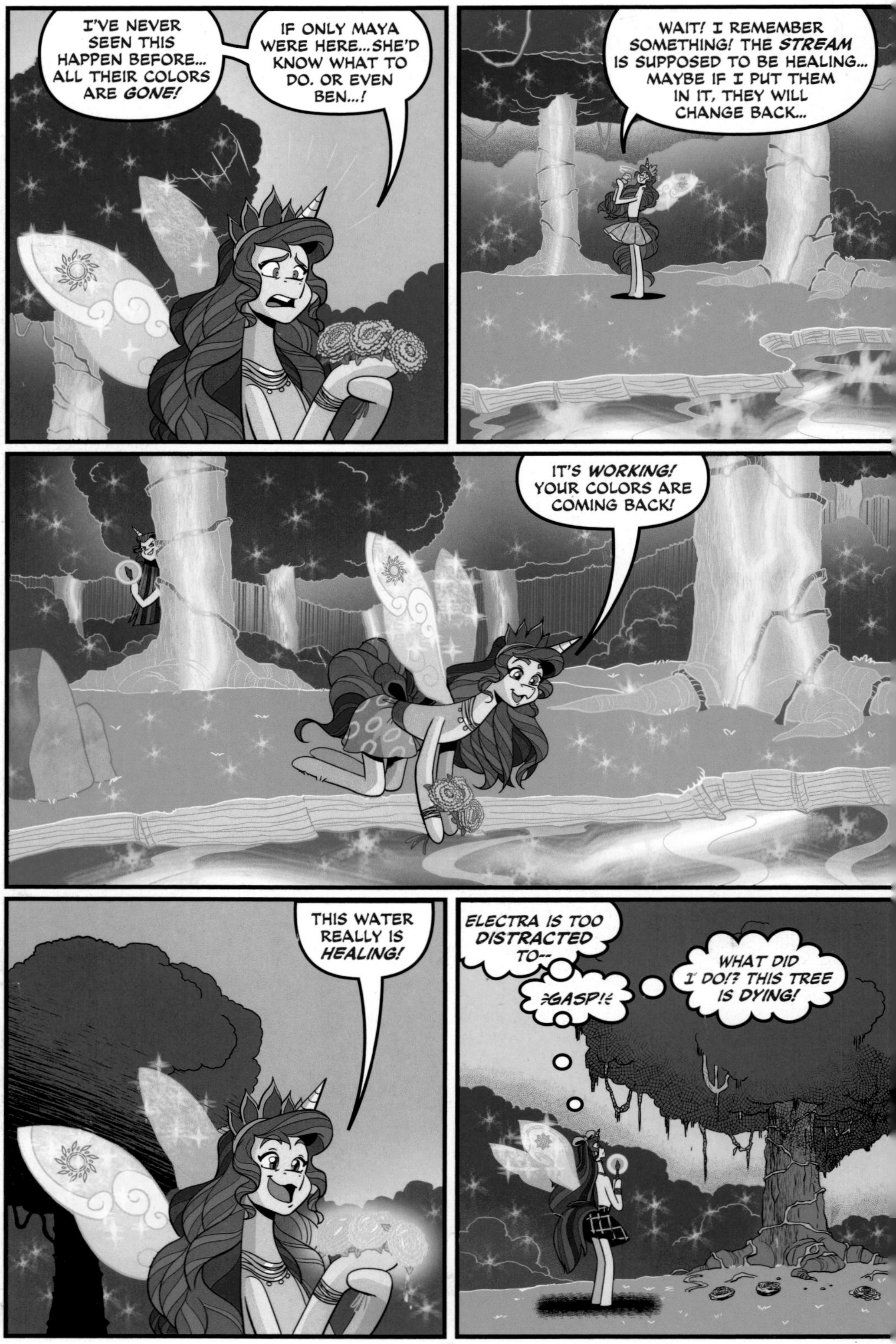

I'VE NEVER SEEN THIS HAPPEN BEFORE... ALL THEIR COLORS ARE *GONE!*
IF ONLY MAYA WERE HERE...SHE'D KNOW WHAT TO DO. OR EVEN BEN...!
WAIT! I REMEMBER SOMETHING! THE *STREAM* IS SUPPOSED TO BE HEALING... MAYBE IF I PUT THEM IN IT, THEY WILL CHANGE BACK...
IT'S *WORKING!* YOUR COLORS ARE COMING BACK!
THIS WATER REALLY IS *HEALING!*
ELECTRA IS TOO *DISTRACTED* TO--
GASP!
WHAT DID *I* DO!? THIS TREE IS *DYING!*

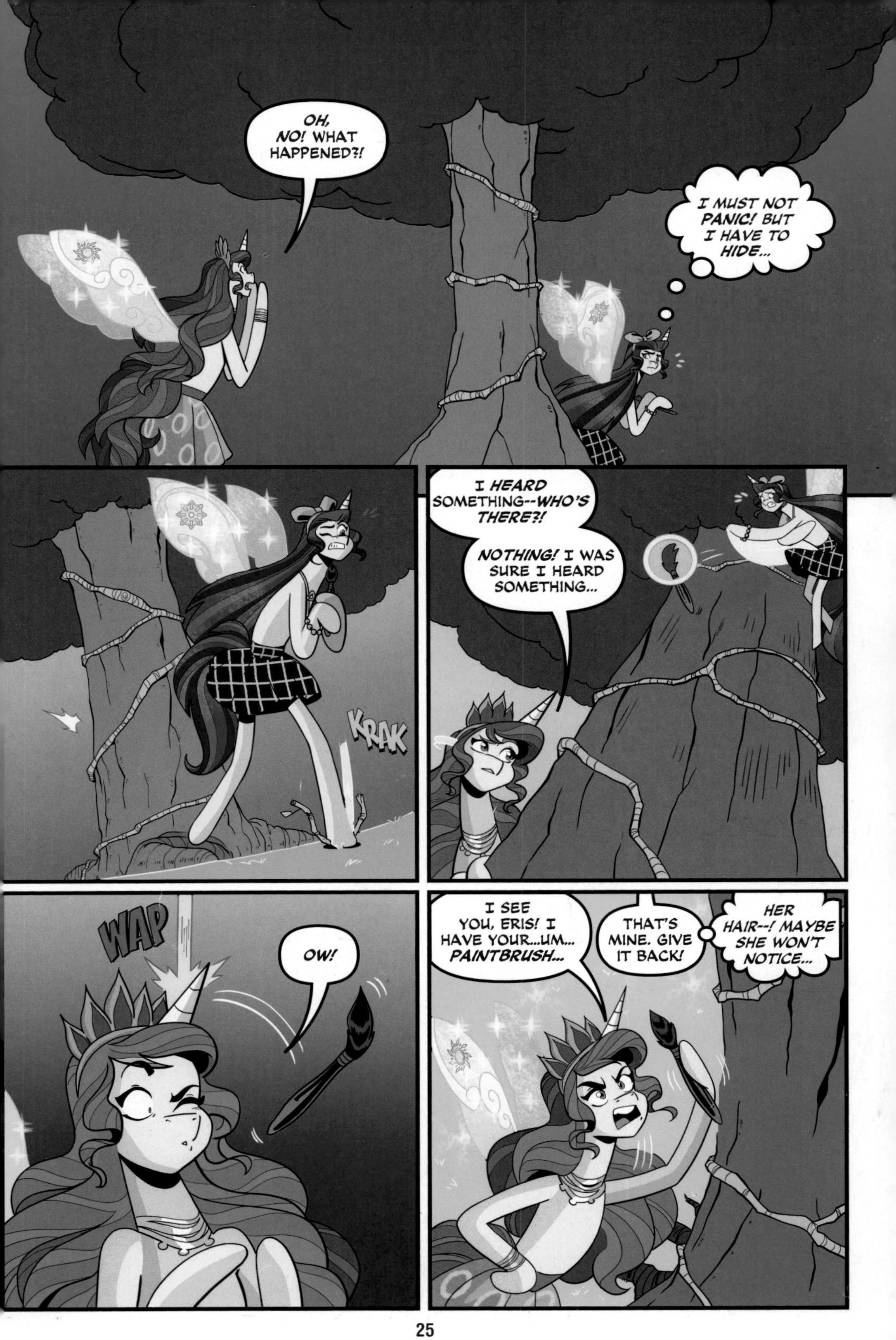
OH, NO! WHAT HAPPENED?!
I MUST NOT PANIC! BUT I HAVE TO HIDE...
KRAK
I HEARD SOMETHING--WHO'S THERE?!
NOTHING! I WAS SURE I HEARD SOMETHING...
WAP
OW!
I SEE YOU, ERIS! I HAVE YOUR...UM... PAINTBRUSH...
THAT'S MINE. GIVE IT BACK!
HER HAIR--! MAYBE SHE WON'T NOTICE...

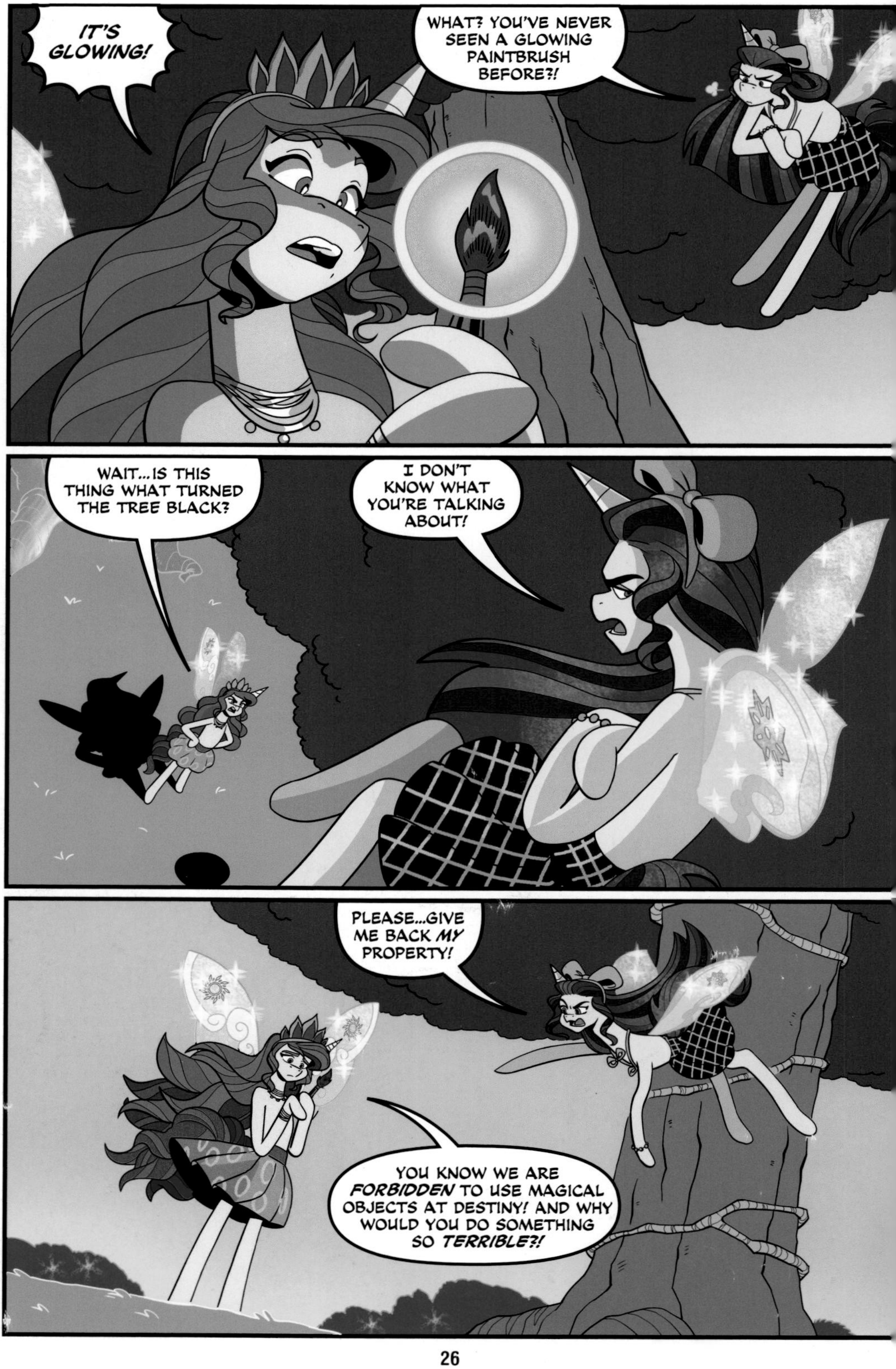
IT'S GLOWING!
WHAT? YOU'VE NEVER SEEN A GLOWING PAINTBRUSH BEFORE?!
WAIT...IS THIS THING WHAT TURNED THE TREE BLACK?
I DON'T KNOW WHAT YOU'RE TALKING ABOUT!
PLEASE...GIVE ME BACK MY PROPERTY!
YOU KNOW WE ARE FORBIDDEN TO USE MAGICAL OBJECTS AT DESTINY! AND WHY WOULD YOU DO SOMETHING SO TERRIBLE?!

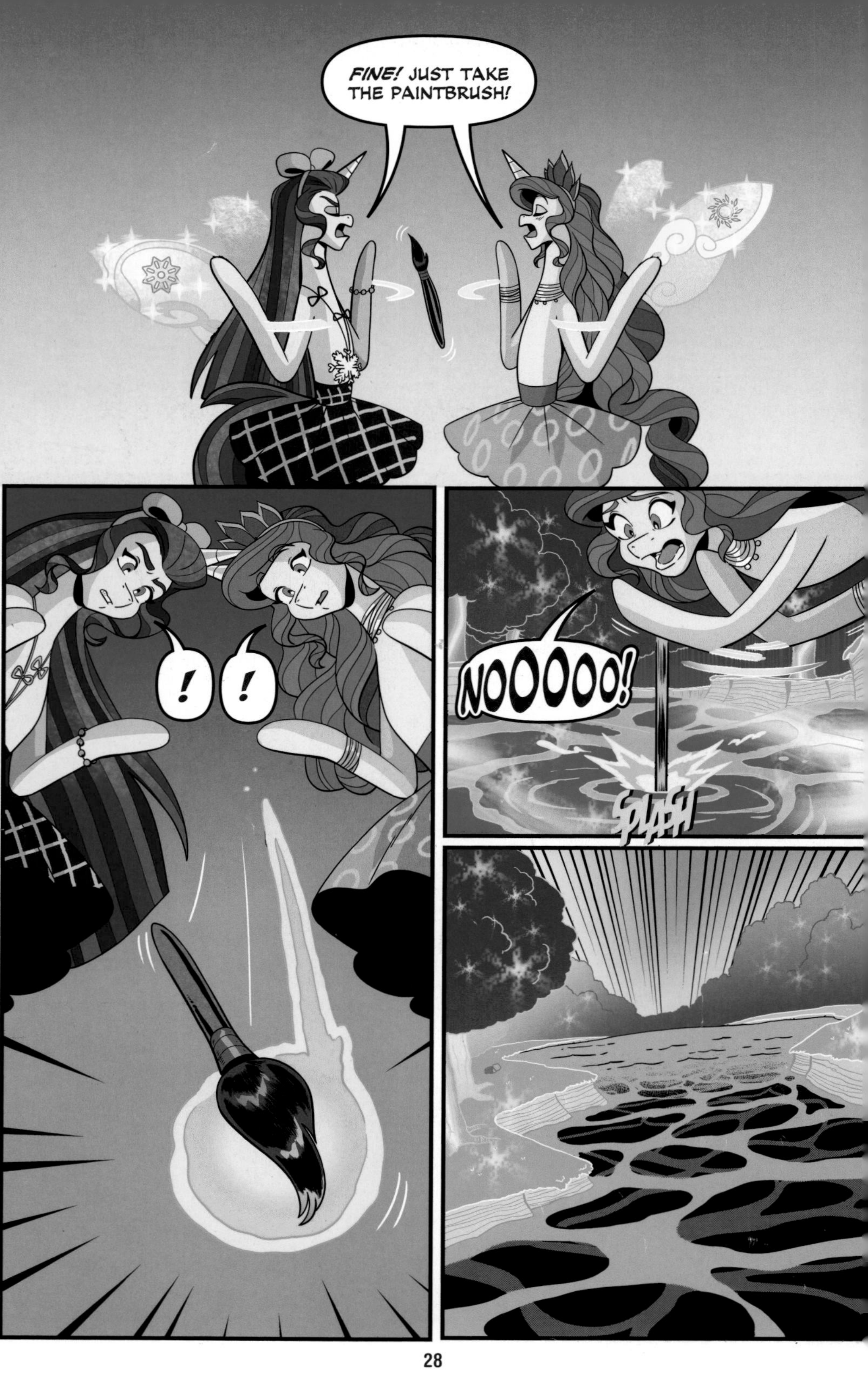
FINE! JUST TAKE
THE PAINTBRUSH!
!
!
NOOOOO!
SPLASH

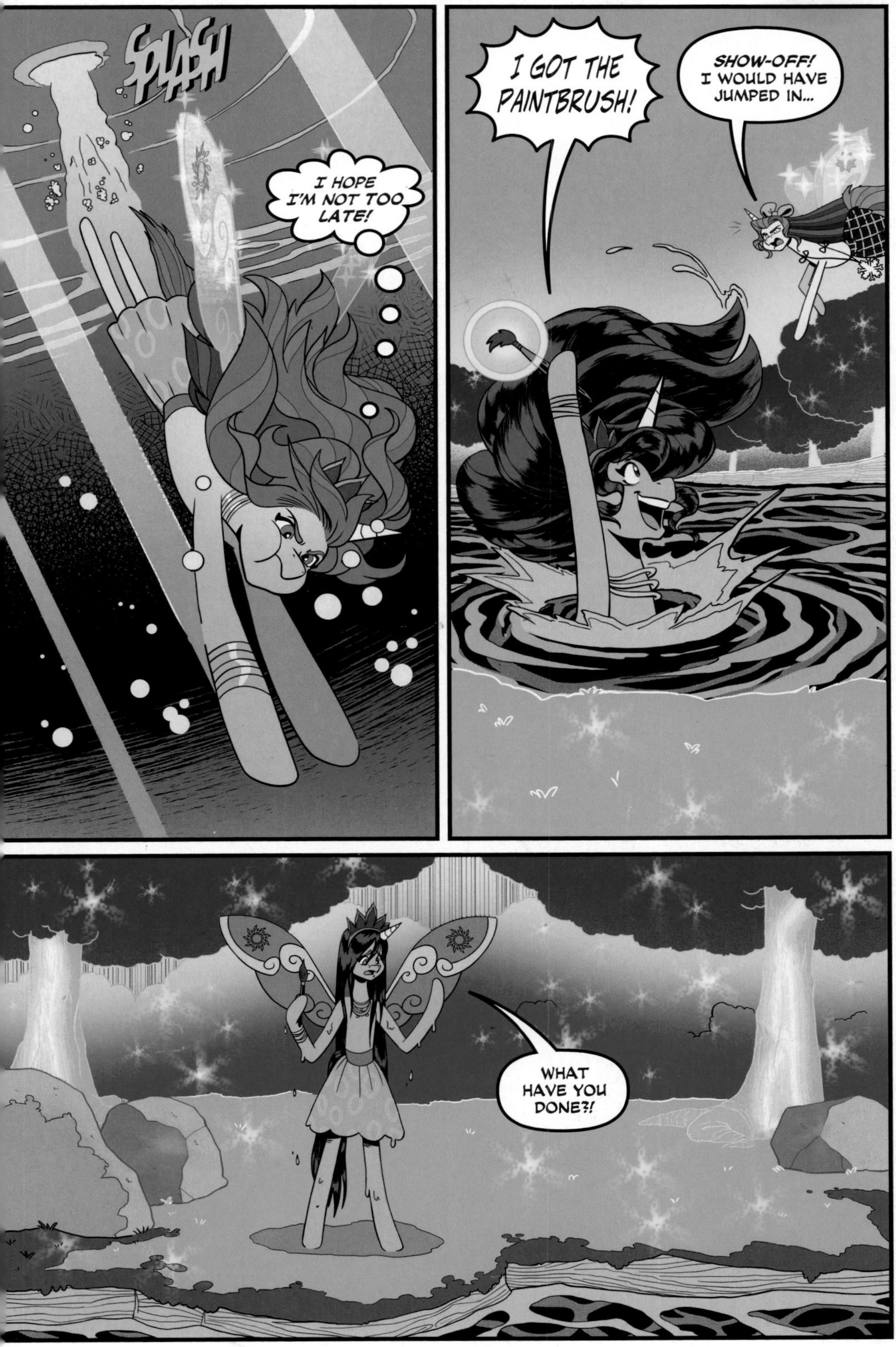
SPLASH
I HOPE I'M NOT TOO LATE!
I GOT THE PAINTBRUSH!
SHOW-OFF! I WOULD HAVE JUMPED IN...
WHAT HAVE YOU DONE?!

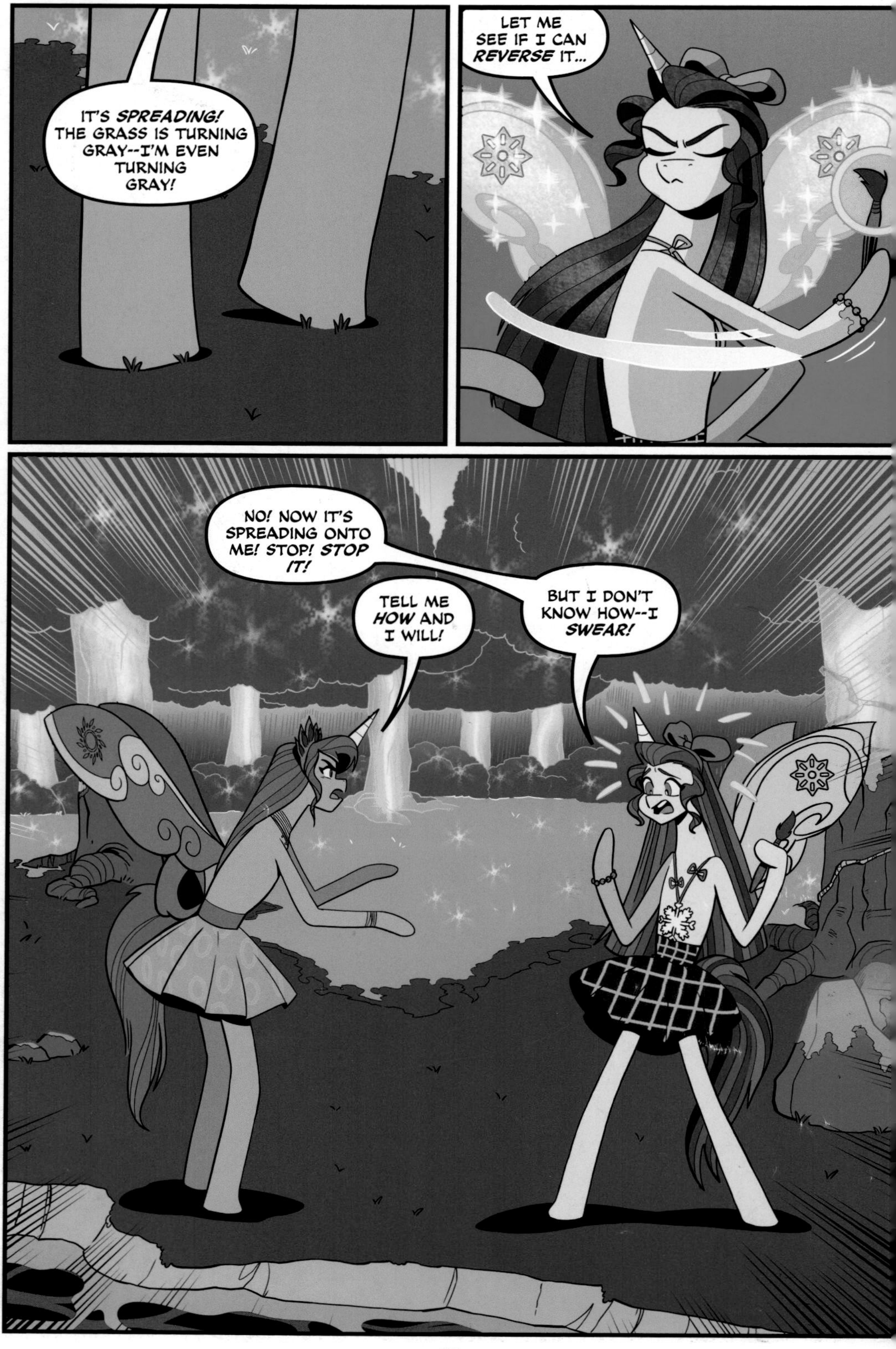
IT'S SPREADING! THE GRASS IS TURNING GRAY--I'M EVEN TURNING GRAY!
LET ME SEE IF I CAN REVERSE IT...
NO! NOW IT'S SPREADING ONTO ME! STOP! STOP IT!
TELL ME HOW AND I WILL!
BUT I DON'T KNOW HOW--I SWEAR!

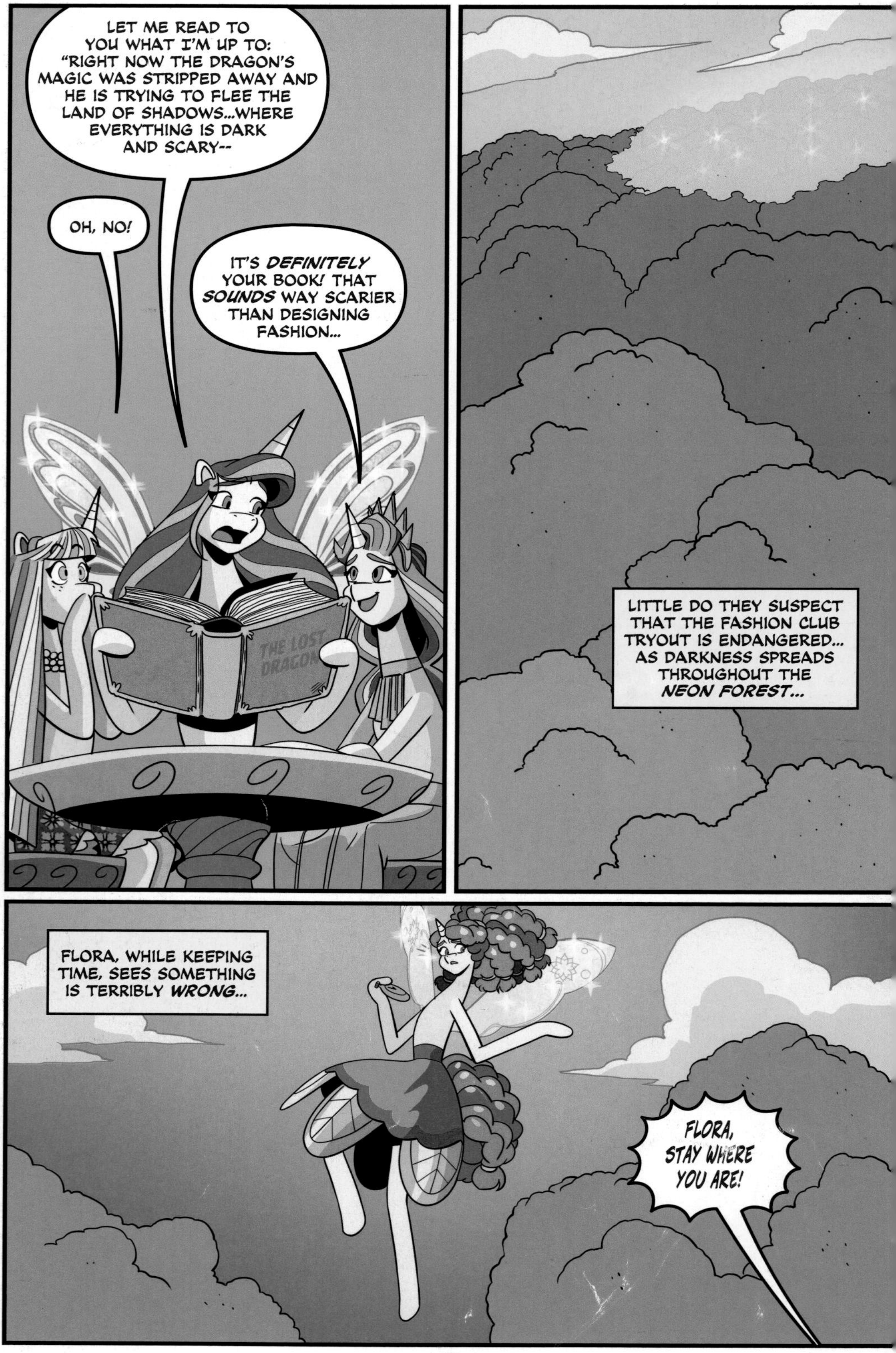
LET ME READ TO YOU WHAT I'M UP TO: "RIGHT NOW THE DRAGON'S MAGIC WAS STRIPPED AWAY AND HE IS TRYING TO FLEE THE LAND OF SHADOWS...WHERE EVERYTHING IS DARK AND SCARY--
OH, NO!
IT'S DEFINITELY YOUR BOOK! THAT SOUNDS WAY SCARIER THAN DESIGNING FASHION...
THE LOST DRAGON
LITTLE DO THEY SUSPECT THAT THE FASHION CLUB TRYOUT IS ENDANGERED... AS DARKNESS SPREADS THROUGHOUT THE NEON FOREST...
FLORA, WHILE KEEPING TIME, SEES SOMETHING IS TERRIBLY WRONG...
FLORA, STAY WHERE YOU ARE!

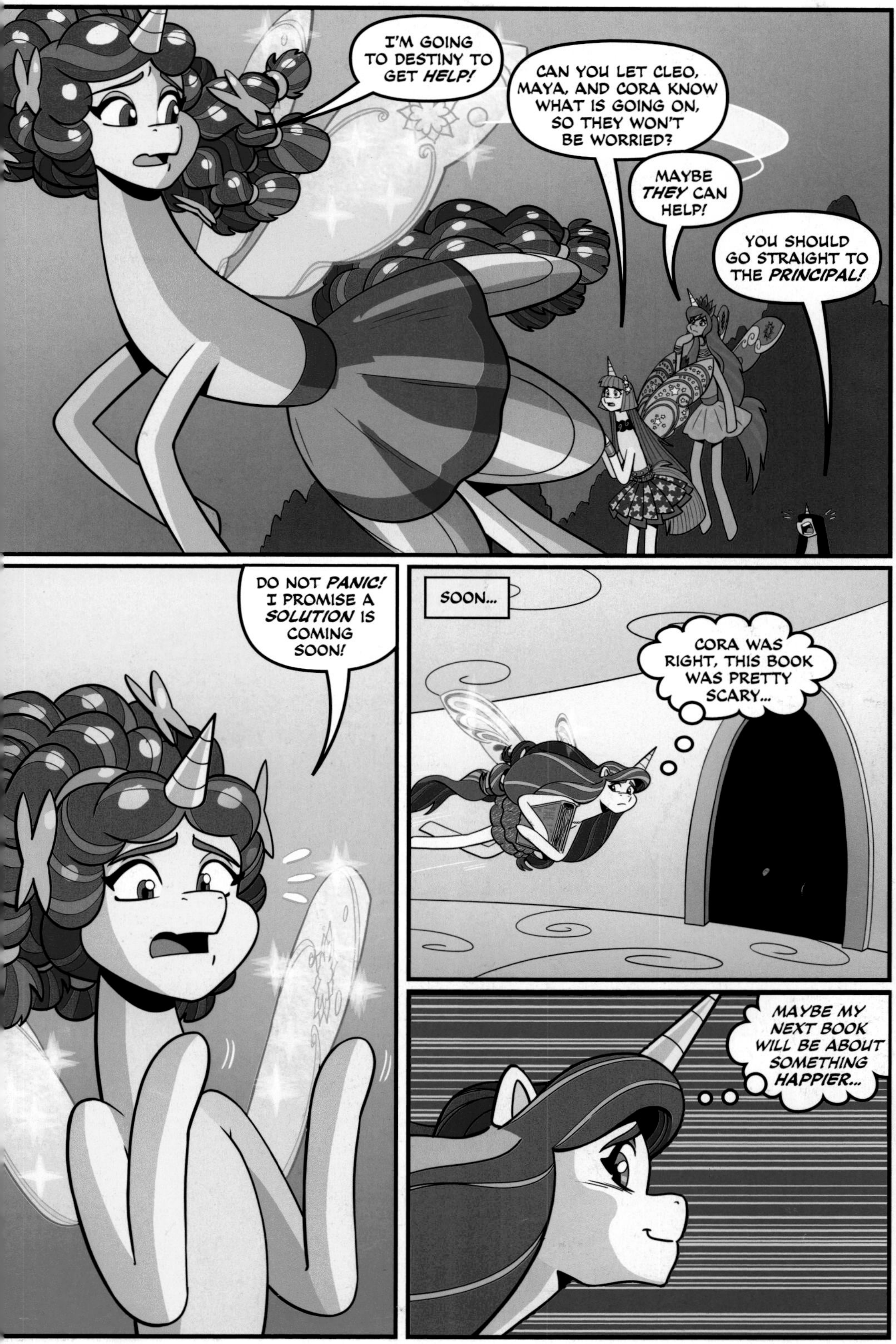
I'M GOING TO DESTINY TO GET *HELP!*
CAN YOU LET CLEO, MAYA, AND CORA KNOW WHAT IS GOING ON, SO THEY WON'T BE WORRIED?
MAYBE *THEY* CAN HELP!
YOU SHOULD GO STRAIGHT TO THE *PRINCIPAL!*
DO NOT *PANIC!* I PROMISE A *SOLUTION* IS COMING SOON!
SOON...
CORA WAS RIGHT, THIS BOOK WAS PRETTY SCARY...
MAYBE MY NEXT BOOK WILL BE ABOUT SOMETHING HAPPIER...

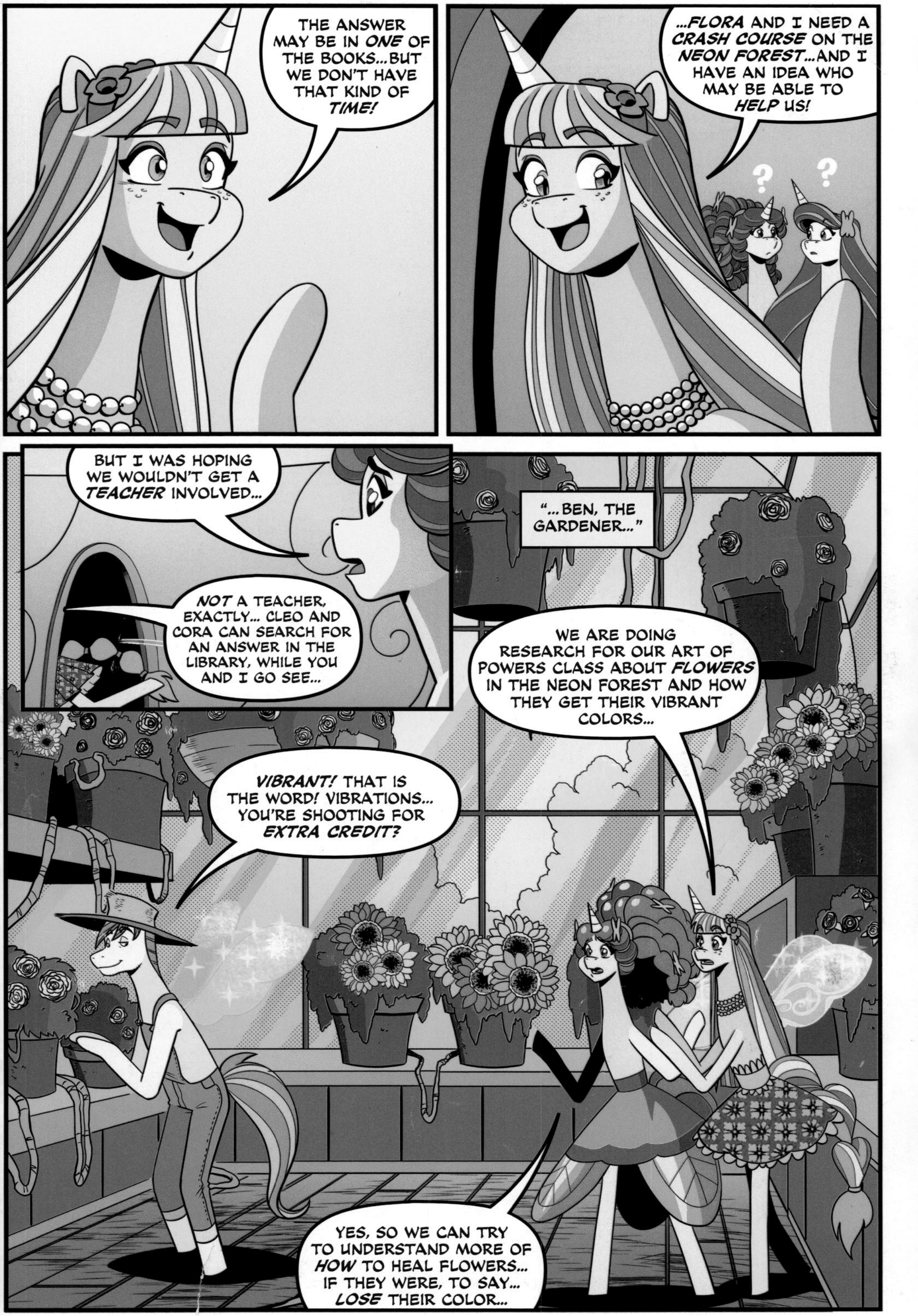
THE ANSWER MAY BE IN *ONE* OF THE BOOKS...BUT WE DON'T HAVE THAT KIND OF *TIME!*
...*FLORA* AND I NEED A *CRASH COURSE* ON THE *NEON FOREST*...AND I HAVE AN IDEA WHO MAY BE ABLE TO *HELP* US!
?
?
BUT I WAS HOPING WE WOULDN'T GET A *TEACHER* INVOLVED...
NOT A TEACHER, EXACTLY... CLEO AND CORA CAN SEARCH FOR AN ANSWER IN THE LIBRARY, WHILE YOU AND I GO SEE...
"...BEN, THE GARDENER..."
WE ARE DOING RESEARCH FOR OUR ART OF POWERS CLASS ABOUT *FLOWERS* IN THE NEON FOREST AND HOW THEY GET THEIR VIBRANT COLORS...
VIBRANT! THAT IS THE WORD! VIBRATIONS... YOU'RE SHOOTING FOR *EXTRA CREDIT?*
YES, SO WE CAN TRY TO UNDERSTAND MORE OF *HOW* TO HEAL FLOWERS... IF THEY WERE, TO SAY... *LOSE* THEIR COLOR...

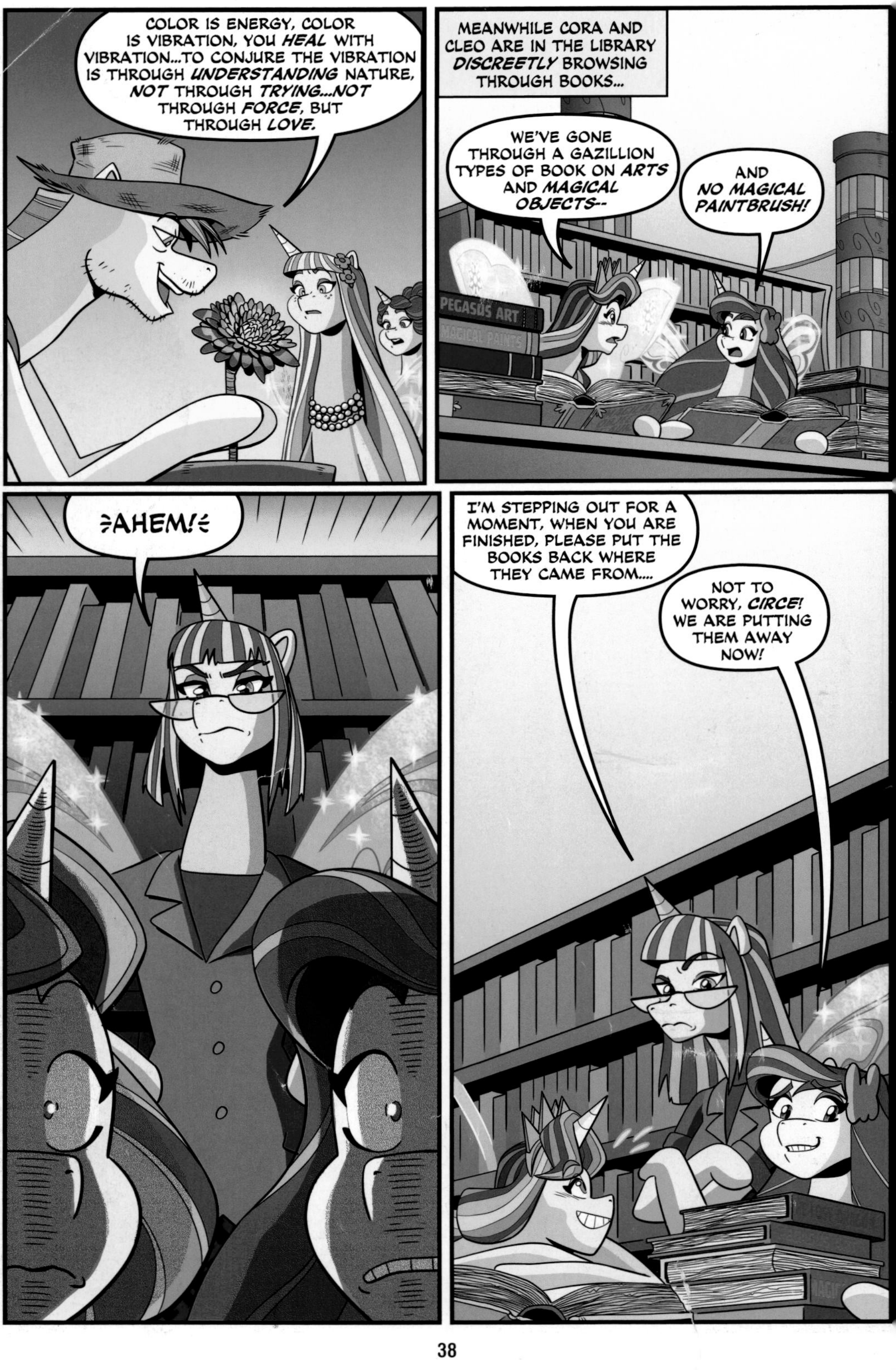
COLOR IS ENERGY, COLOR IS VIBRATION, YOU *HEAL* WITH VIBRATION...TO CONJURE THE VIBRATION IS THROUGH *UNDERSTANDING* NATURE, *NOT* THROUGH *TRYING*...*NOT* THROUGH *FORCE*, BUT THROUGH *LOVE*.
MEANWHILE CORA AND CLEO ARE IN THE LIBRARY *DISCREETLY* BROWSING THROUGH BOOKS...
WE'VE GONE THROUGH A GAZILLION TYPES OF BOOK ON *ARTS* AND *MAGICAL OBJECTS*--
AND *NO MAGICAL PAINTBRUSH!*
PEGASUS ART
MAGICAL PAINTS
AHEM!
I'M STEPPING OUT FOR A MOMENT, WHEN YOU ARE FINISHED, PLEASE PUT THE BOOKS BACK WHERE THEY CAME FROM....
NOT TO WORRY, *CIRCE*! WE ARE PUTTING THEM AWAY NOW!

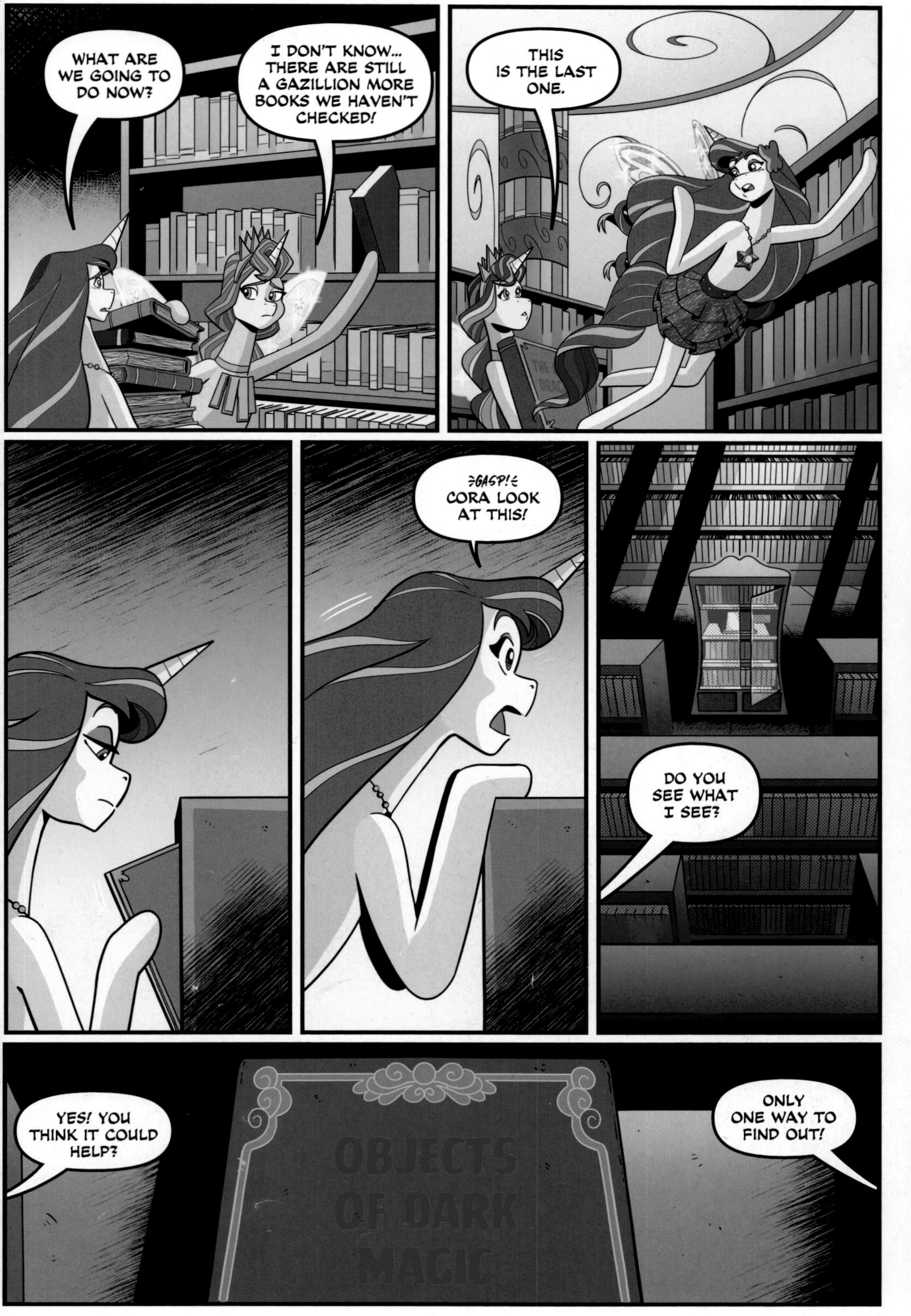
WHAT ARE WE GOING TO DO NOW?
I DON'T KNOW... THERE ARE STILL A GAZILLION MORE BOOKS WE HAVEN'T CHECKED!
THIS IS THE LAST ONE.
GASP! CORA LOOK AT THIS!
DO YOU SEE WHAT I SEE?
YES! YOU THINK IT COULD HELP?
OBJECTS OF DARK MAGIC
ONLY ONE WAY TO FIND OUT!

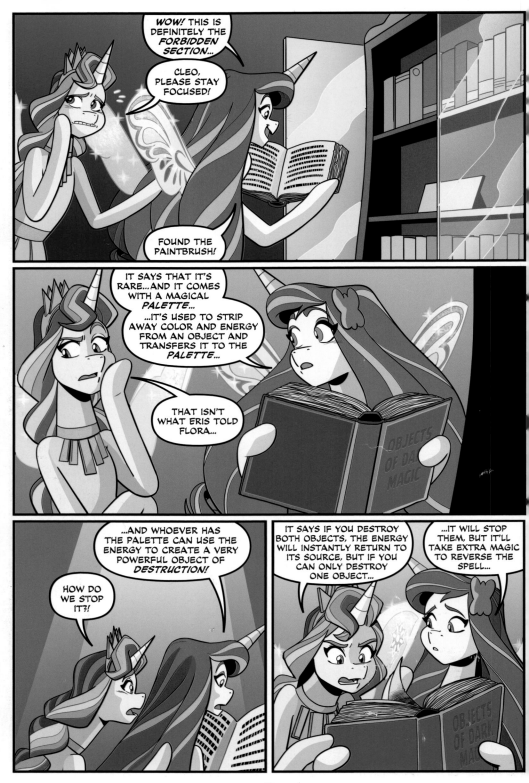

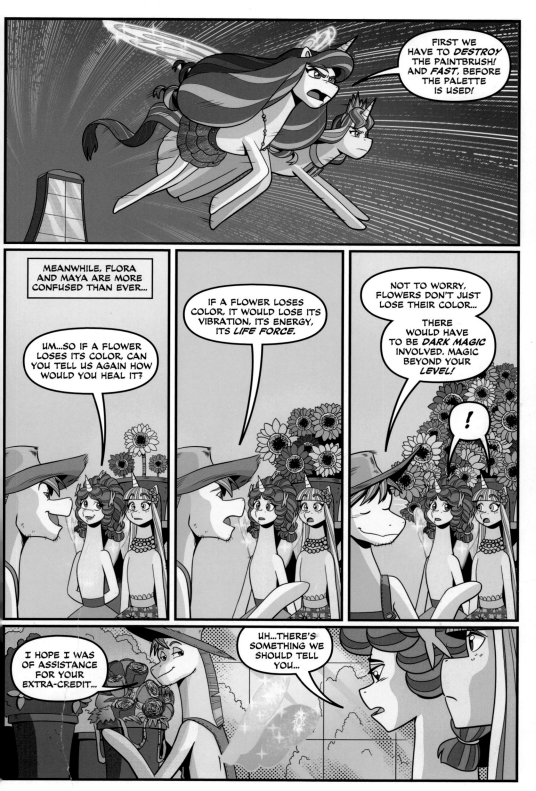

FIRST WE HAVE TO *DESTROY* THE PAINTBRUSH! AND *FAST,* BEFORE THE PALETTE IS USED!

MEANWHILE, FLORA AND MAYA ARE MORE CONFUSED THAN EVER...

UM...SO IF A FLOWER LOSES ITS COLOR, CAN YOU TELL US AGAIN HOW WOULD YOU HEAL IT?

IF A FLOWER LOSES COLOR, IT WOULD LOSE ITS VIBRATION, ITS ENERGY, ITS *LIFE FORCE.*

NOT TO WORRY, FLOWERS DON'T JUST LOSE THEIR COLOR...

THERE WOULD HAVE TO BE *DARK MAGIC* INVOLVED. MAGIC BEYOND YOUR *LEVEL!*

!

I HOPE I WAS OF ASSISTANCE FOR YOUR EXTRA-CREDIT...

UH...THERE'S SOMETHING WE SHOULD TELL YOU...

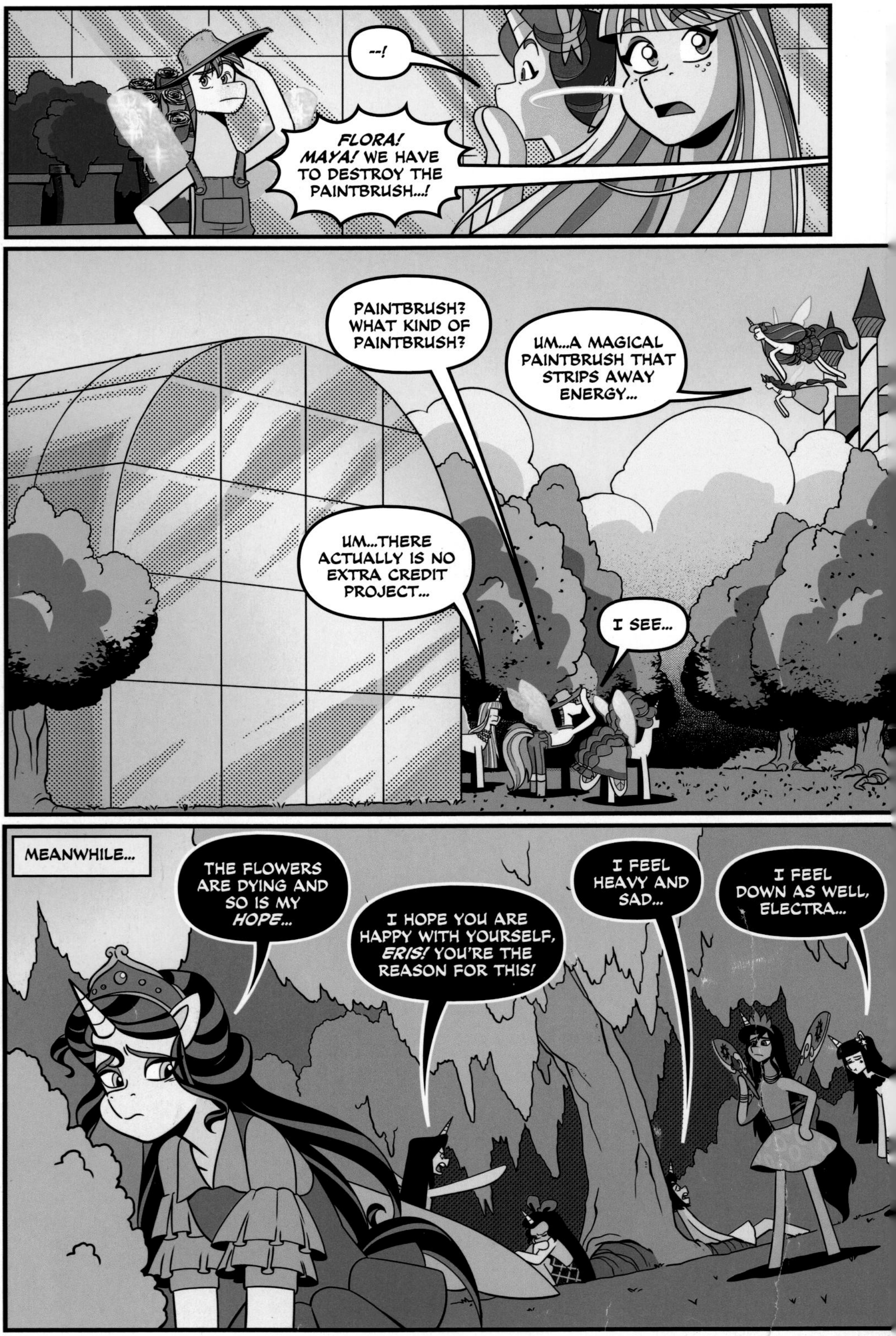

--!
FLORA! MAYA! WE HAVE TO DESTROY THE PAINTBRUSH...!
PAINTBRUSH? WHAT KIND OF PAINTBRUSH?
UM...A MAGICAL PAINTBRUSH THAT STRIPS AWAY ENERGY...
UM...THERE ACTUALLY IS NO EXTRA CREDIT PROJECT...
I SEE...
MEANWHILE...
THE FLOWERS ARE DYING AND SO IS MY HOPE...
I HOPE YOU ARE HAPPY WITH YOURSELF, ERIS! YOU'RE THE REASON FOR THIS!
I FEEL HEAVY AND SAD...
I FEEL DOWN AS WELL, ELECTRA...

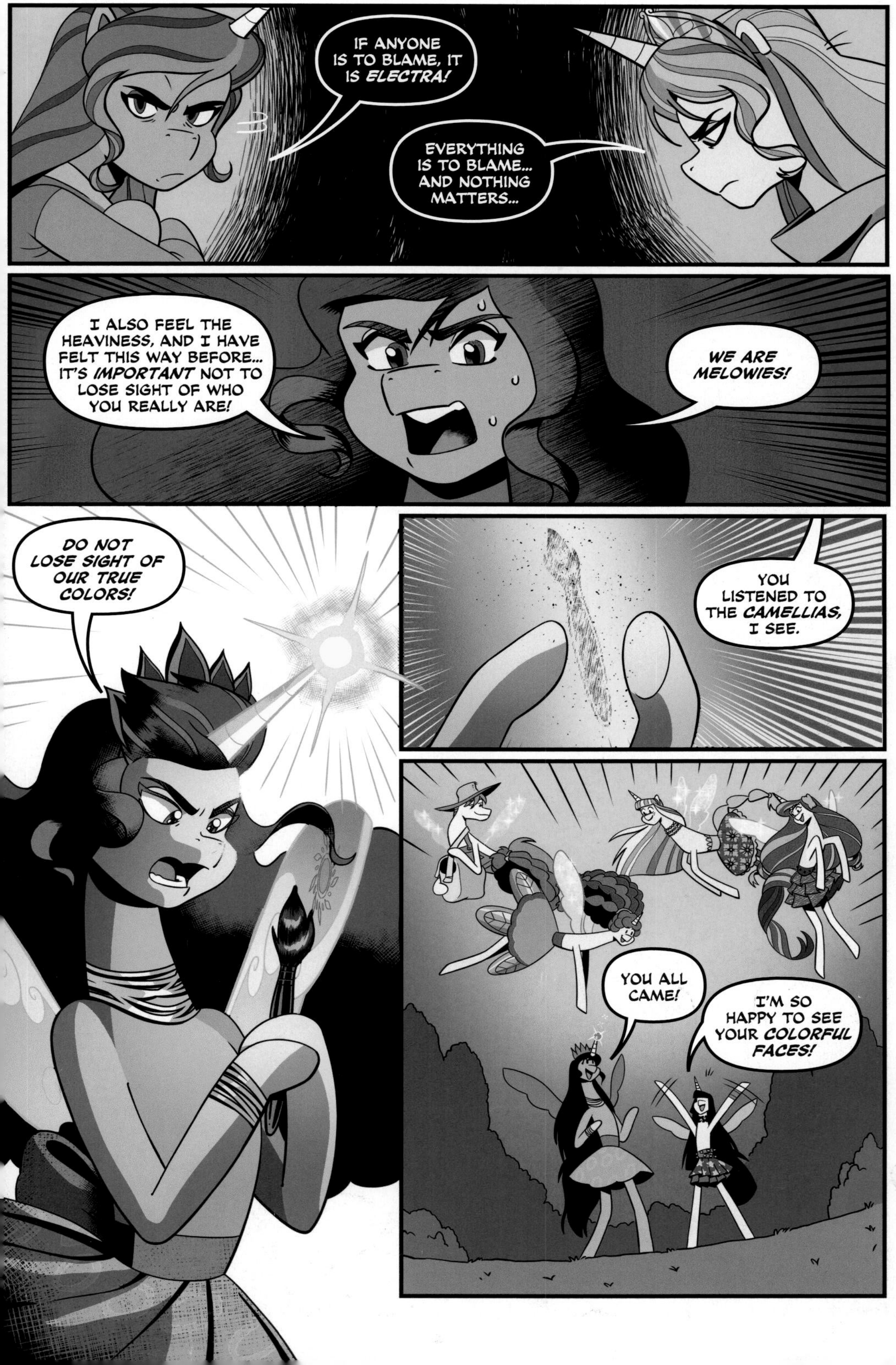
IF ANYONE IS TO BLAME, IT IS *ELECTRA!*
EVERYTHING IS TO BLAME... AND NOTHING MATTERS...
I ALSO FEEL THE HEAVINESS, AND I HAVE FELT THIS WAY BEFORE... IT'S *IMPORTANT* NOT TO LOSE SIGHT OF WHO YOU REALLY ARE!
WE ARE MELOWIES!
DO NOT LOSE SIGHT OF OUR TRUE COLORS!
YOU LISTENED TO THE *CAMELLIAS,* I SEE.
YOU ALL CAME!
I'M SO HAPPY TO SEE YOUR *COLORFUL FACES!*

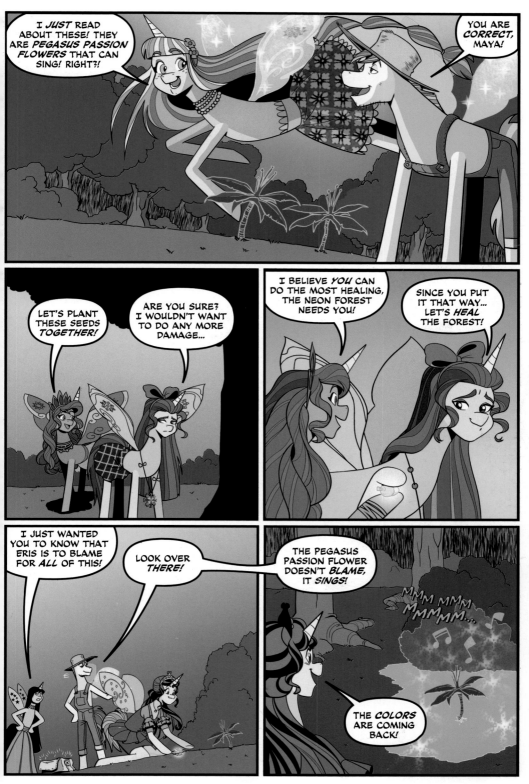

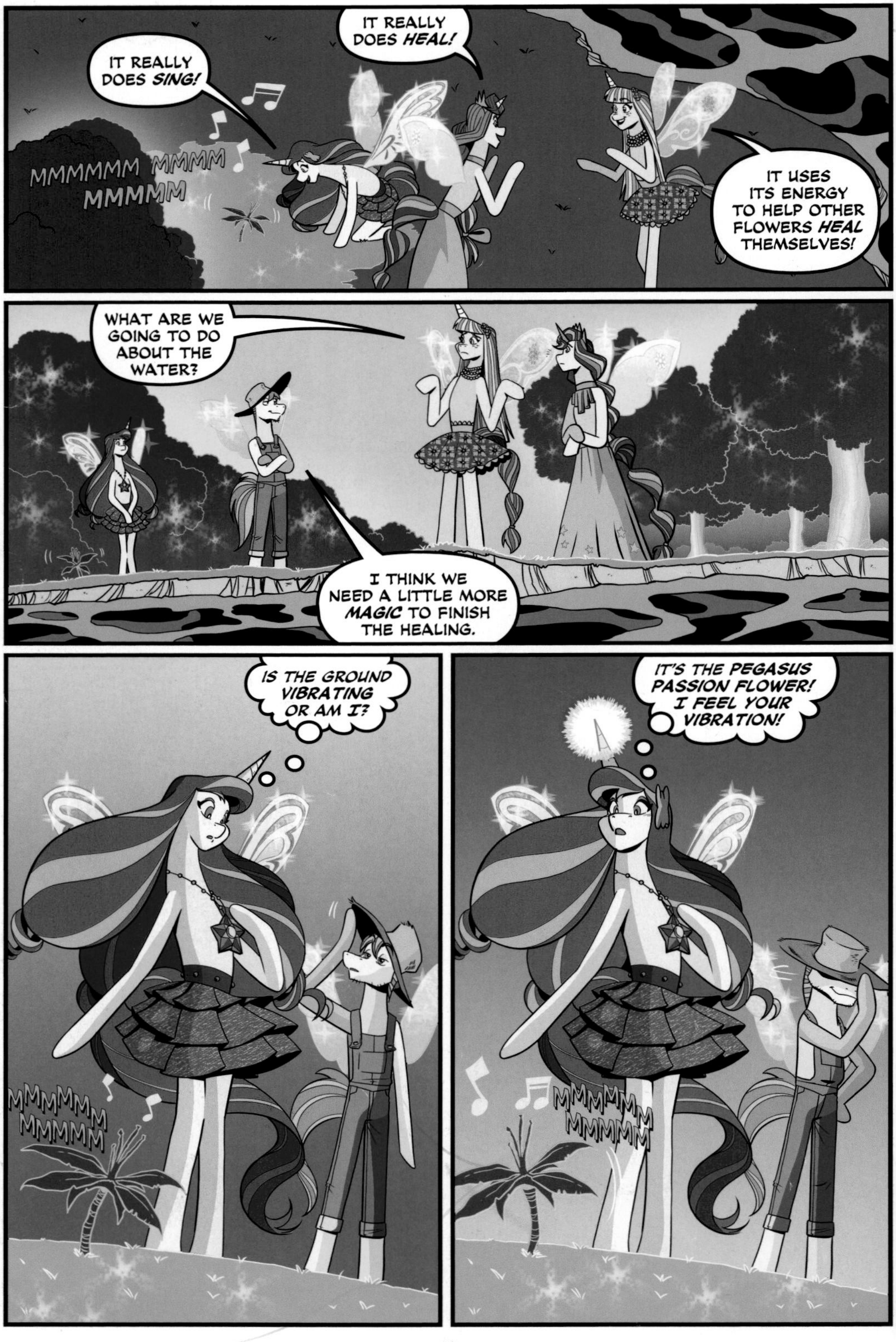
IT REALLY DOES SING!
IT REALLY DOES HEAL!
MMMMMM MMMM MMMMM
IT USES ITS ENERGY TO HELP OTHER FLOWERS HEAL THEMSELVES!
WHAT ARE WE GOING TO DO ABOUT THE WATER?
I THINK WE NEED A LITTLE MORE MAGIC TO FINISH THE HEALING.
IS THE GROUND VIBRATING OR AM I?
MMMMMM MMMMM
IT'S THE PEGASUS PASSION FLOWER! I FEEL YOUR VIBRATION!
MMMMMM MMMMM

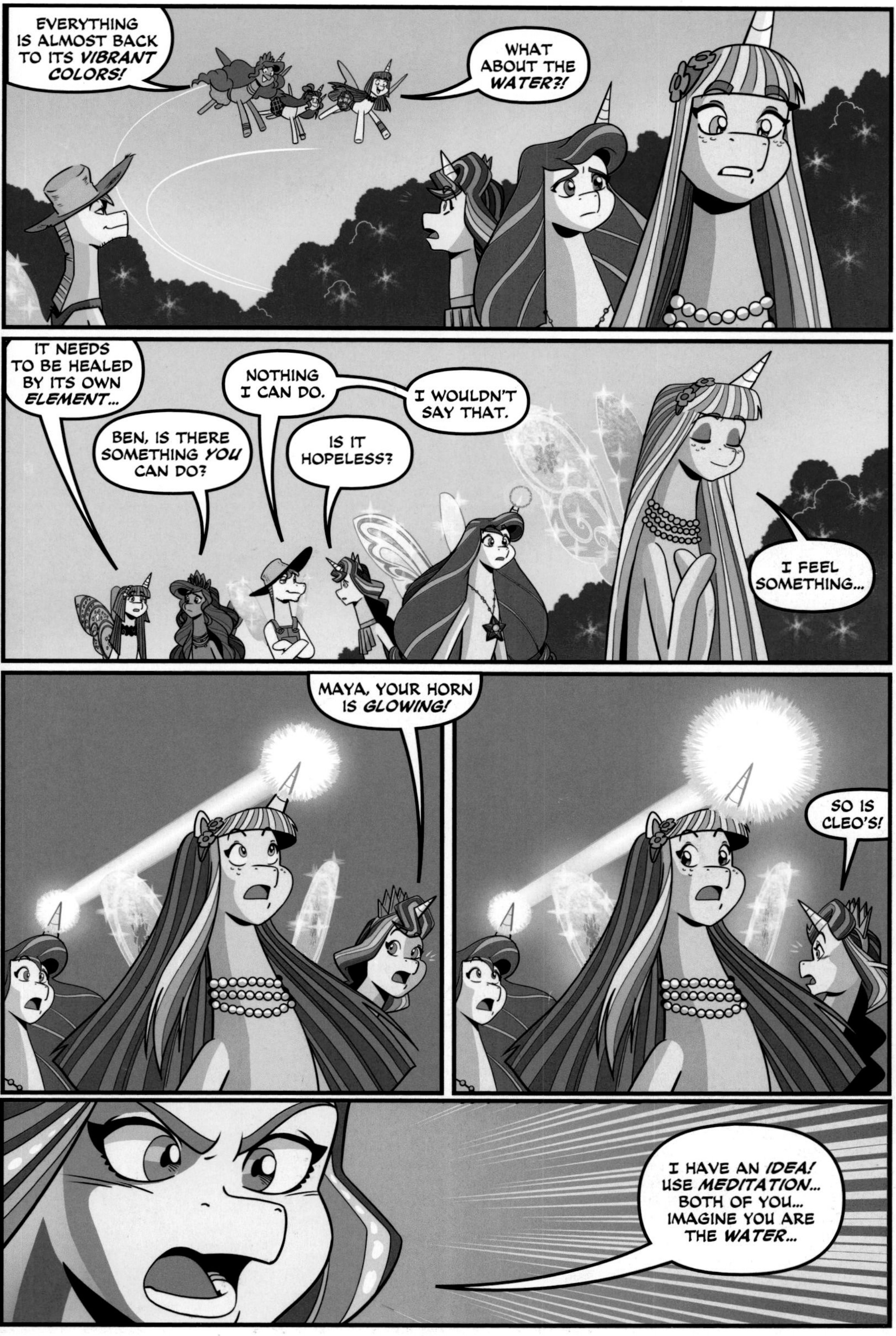
EVERYTHING IS ALMOST BACK TO ITS VIBRANT COLORS!
WHAT ABOUT THE WATER?!
IT NEEDS TO BE HEALED BY ITS OWN ELEMENT...
BEN, IS THERE SOMETHING YOU CAN DO?
NOTHING I CAN DO.
IS IT HOPELESS?
I WOULDN'T SAY THAT.
I FEEL SOMETHING...
MAYA, YOUR HORN IS GLOWING!
SO IS CLEO'S!
I HAVE AN IDEA! USE MEDITATION... BOTH OF YOU... IMAGINE YOU ARE THE WATER...

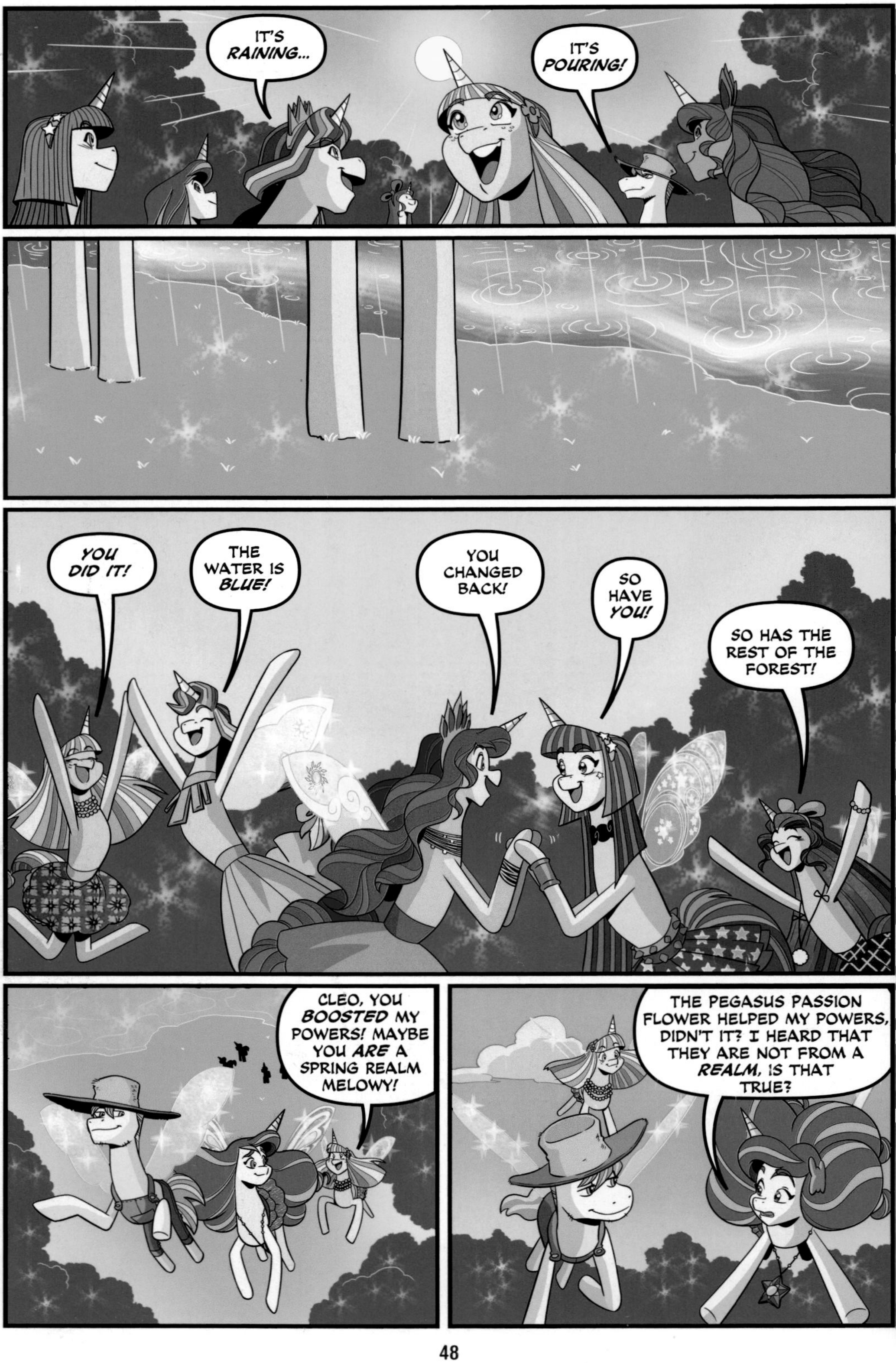
IT'S RAINING...
IT'S POURING!
YOU DID IT!
THE WATER IS BLUE!
YOU CHANGED BACK!
SO HAVE YOU!
SO HAS THE REST OF THE FOREST!
CLEO, YOU BOOSTED MY POWERS! MAYBE YOU ARE A SPRING REALM MELOWY!
THE PEGASUS PASSION FLOWER HELPED MY POWERS, DIDN'T IT? I HEARD THAT THEY ARE NOT FROM A REALM, IS THAT TRUE?

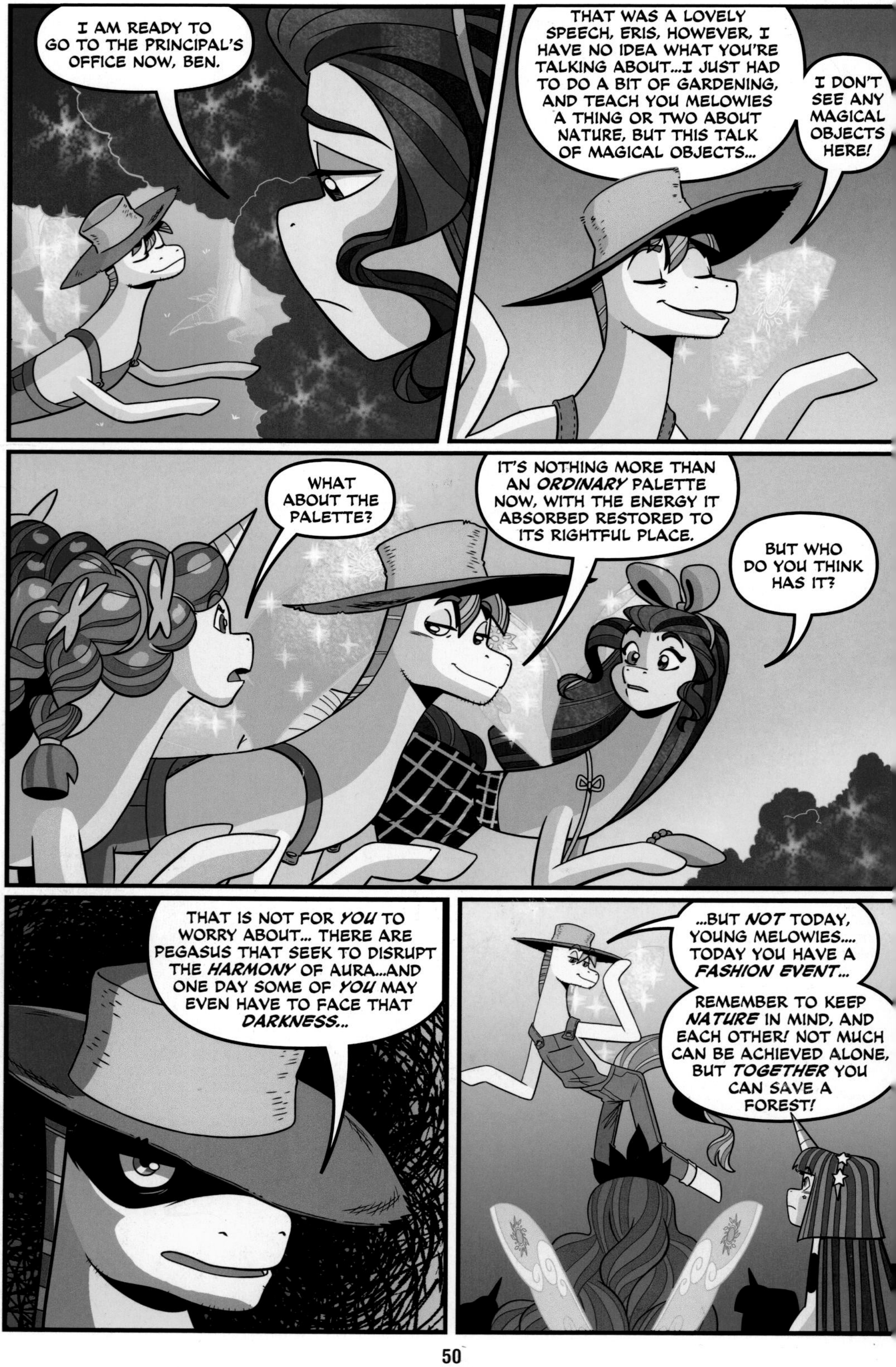

I AM READY TO GO TO THE PRINCIPAL'S OFFICE NOW, BEN.
THAT WAS A LOVELY SPEECH, ERIS, HOWEVER, I HAVE NO IDEA WHAT YOU'RE TALKING ABOUT...I JUST HAD TO DO A BIT OF GARDENING, AND TEACH YOU MELOWIES A THING OR TWO ABOUT NATURE, BUT THIS TALK OF MAGICAL OBJECTS...
I DON'T SEE ANY MAGICAL OBJECTS HERE!
WHAT ABOUT THE PALETTE?
IT'S NOTHING MORE THAN AN *ORDINARY* PALETTE NOW, WITH THE ENERGY IT ABSORBED RESTORED TO ITS RIGHTFUL PLACE.
BUT WHO DO YOU THINK HAS IT?
THAT IS NOT FOR *YOU* TO WORRY ABOUT... THERE ARE PEGASUS THAT SEEK TO DISRUPT THE *HARMONY* OF AURA...AND ONE DAY SOME OF *YOU* MAY EVEN HAVE TO FACE THAT *DARKNESS*...
...BUT *NOT* TODAY, YOUNG MELOWIES.... TODAY YOU HAVE A *FASHION EVENT*...
REMEMBER TO KEEP *NATURE* IN MIND, AND EACH OTHER! NOT MUCH CAN BE ACHIEVED ALONE, BUT *TOGETHER* YOU CAN SAVE A FOREST!

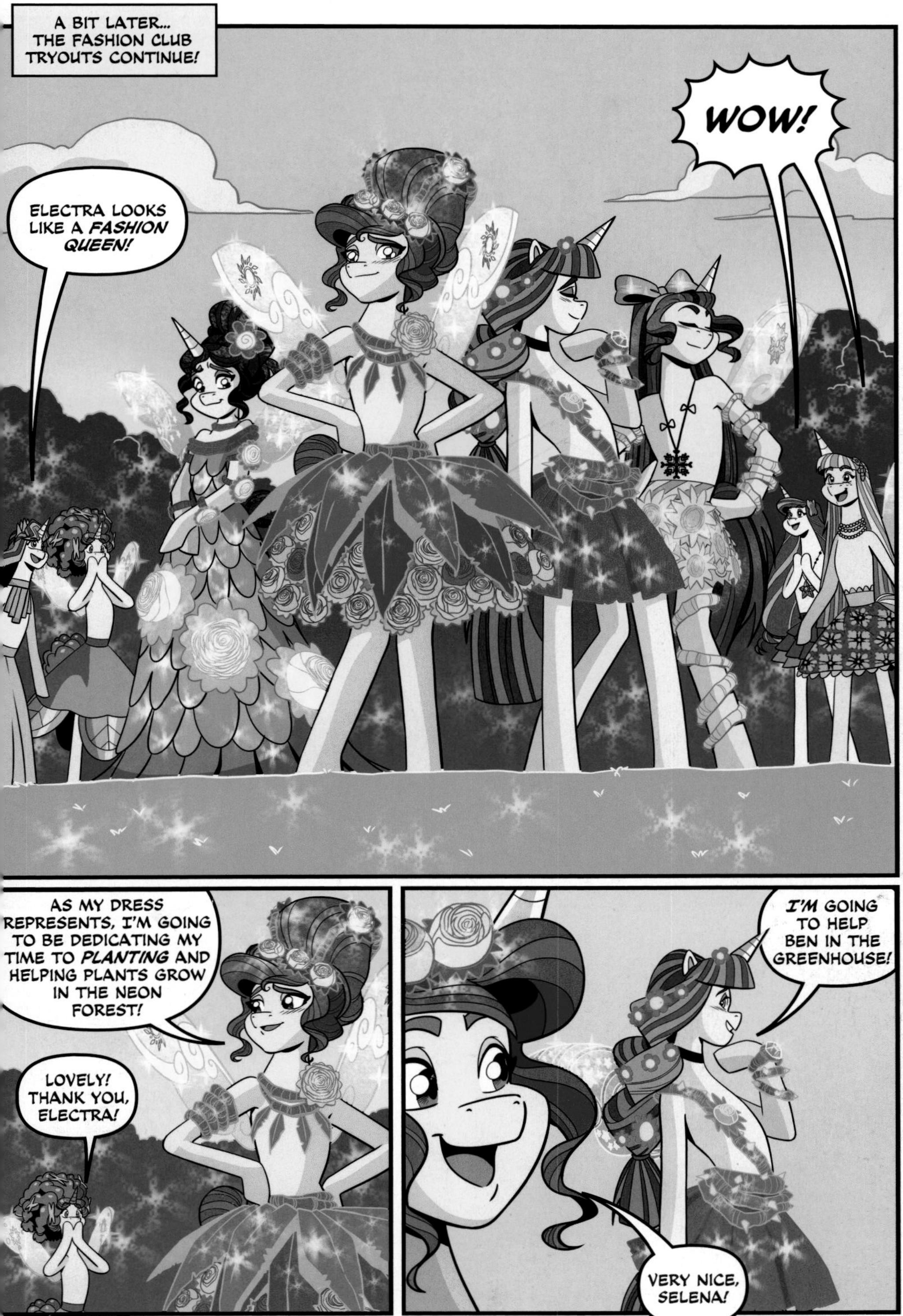
A BIT LATER... THE FASHION CLUB TRYOUTS CONTINUE!
WOW!
ELECTRA LOOKS LIKE A *FASHION QUEEN!*
AS MY DRESS REPRESENTS, I'M GOING TO BE DEDICATING MY TIME TO *PLANTING* AND HELPING PLANTS GROW IN THE NEON FOREST!
LOVELY! THANK YOU, ELECTRA!
I'M GOING TO HELP BEN IN THE GREENHOUSE!
VERY NICE, SELENA!

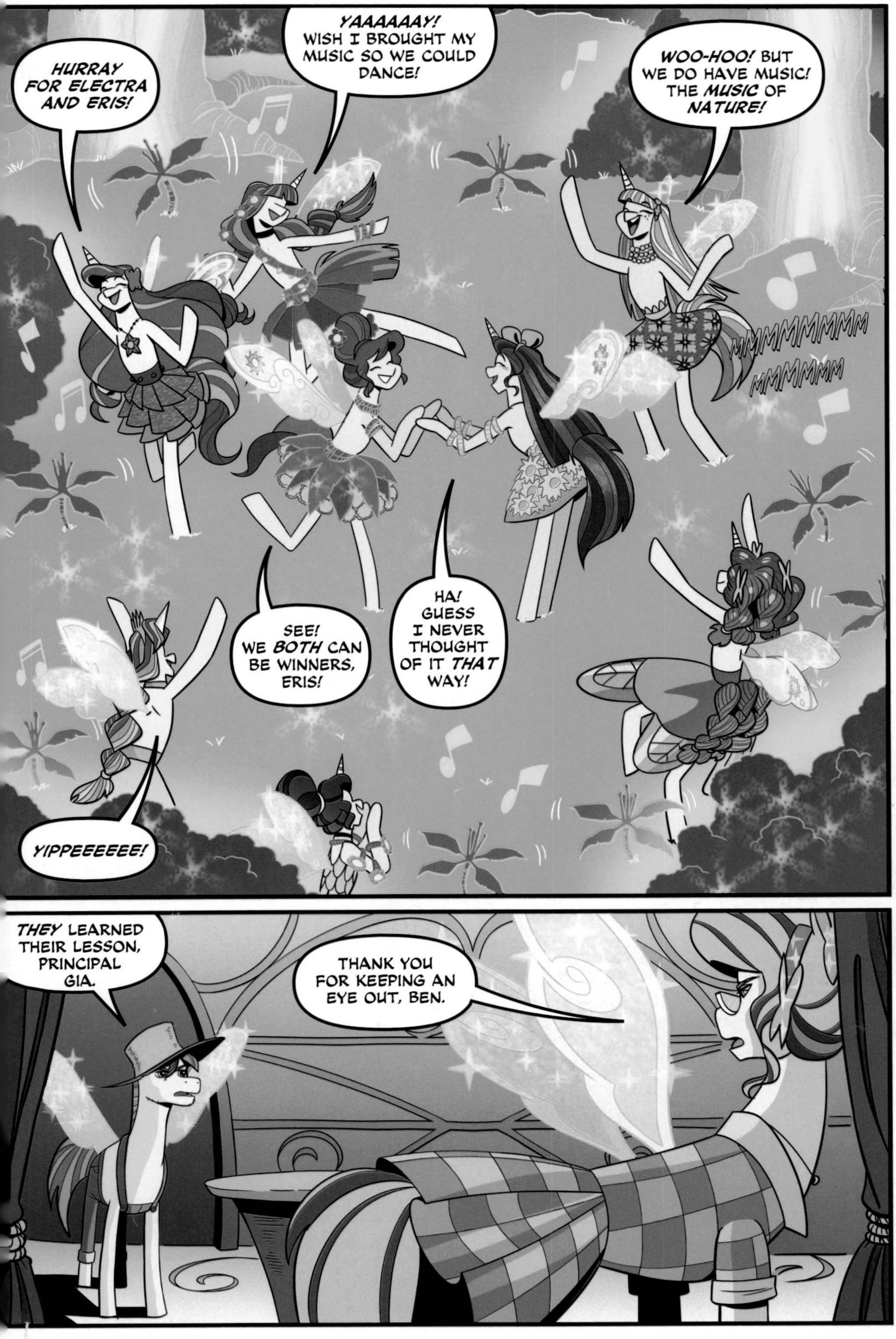
HURRAY FOR ELECTRA AND ERIS!
YAAAAAAY! WISH I BROUGHT MY MUSIC SO WE COULD DANCE!
WOO-HOO! BUT WE DO HAVE MUSIC! THE MUSIC OF NATURE!
MMMMMMMMM
MMMMMMM
SEE! WE BOTH CAN BE WINNERS, ERIS!
HA! GUESS I NEVER THOUGHT OF IT THAT WAY!
YIPPEEEEEE!
THEY LEARNED THEIR LESSON, PRINCIPAL GIA.
THANK YOU FOR KEEPING AN EYE OUT, BEN.

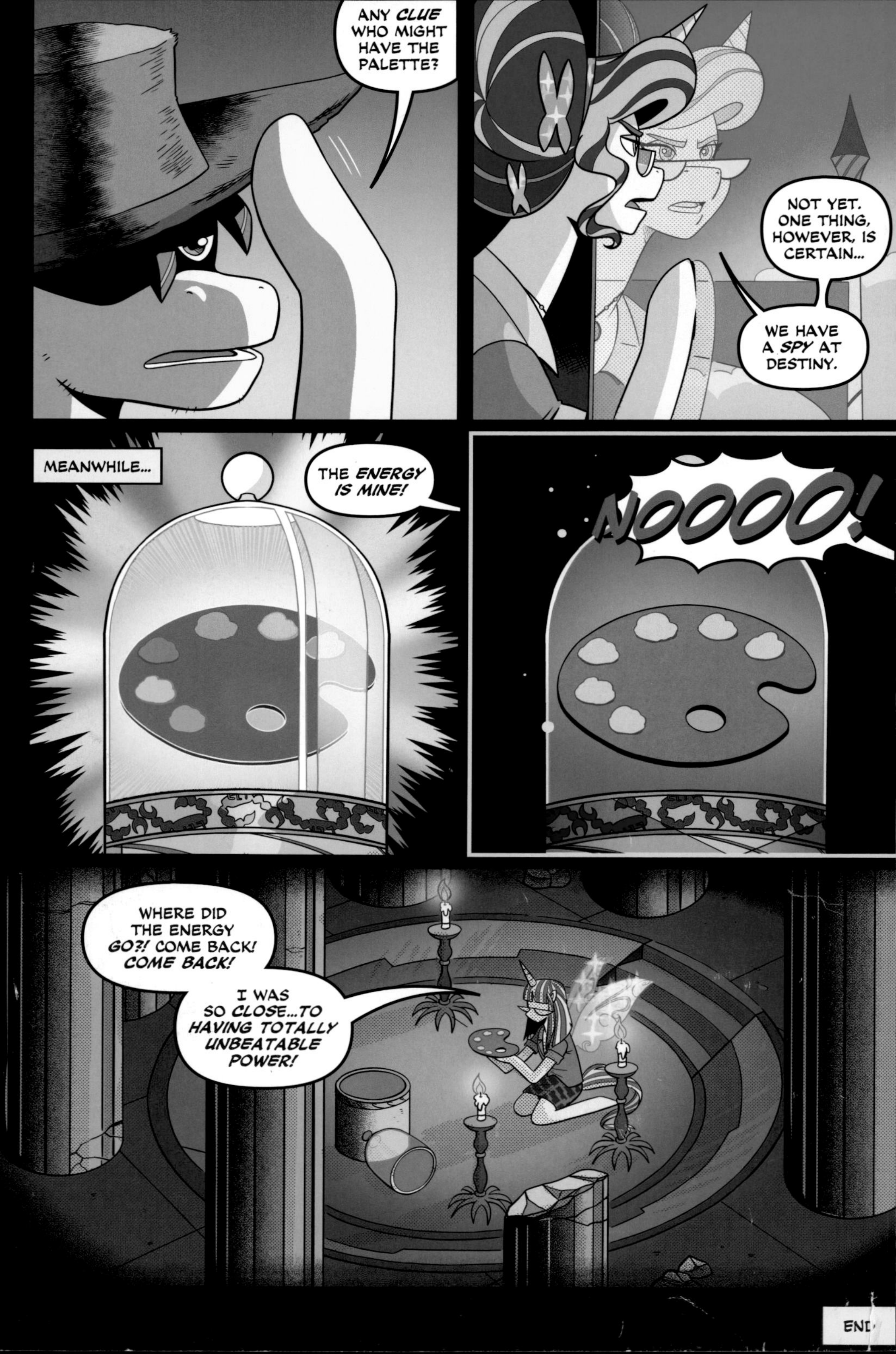
ANY *CLUE* WHO MIGHT HAVE THE PALETTE?
NOT YET. ONE THING, HOWEVER, IS CERTAIN...
WE HAVE A *SPY* AT DESTINY.
MEANWHILE...
THE *ENERGY IS MINE!*
NOOOOO!
WHERE DID THE ENERGY *GO?!* COME BACK! *COME BACK!*
I WAS SO *CLOSE*...TO *HAVING TOTALLY UNBEATABLE POWER!*
END

WATCH OUT FOR PAPERCUTZ™

lcome to the sparkly, second MELOWY graphic novel by Cortney vell and Ryan Jampole based on the characters created by Danielle r, magically brought to you by Papercutz, those enchanting folks licated to publishing graphic novels for all ages. I'm Jim Salicrup, Editor-in-Chief and a Fashion Club reject, here to offer peeks into at's happening in the wonderful world of Papercutz, and maybe n offer a little behind-the-scenes info regarding the creators that g you the MELOWY graphic novels…

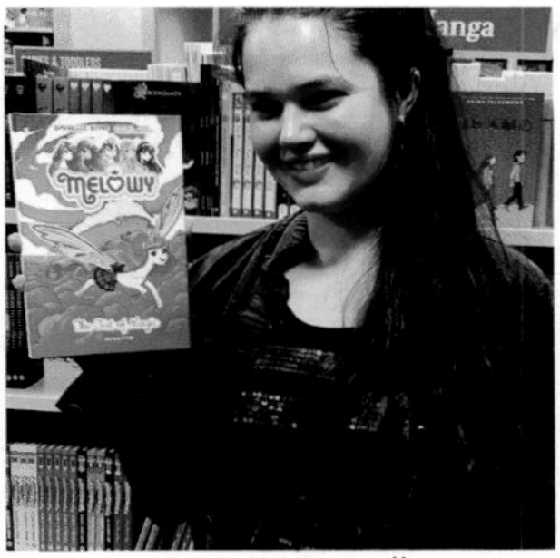

Cortney Powell

LOWY was created by the fascinating nielle Star, and she's also the author of the pter books published by our good friends Scholastic. Danielle Star has done a bit everything. She's been an assistant cook a famous French pastry shop, the head tor of a fashion magazine, and a dance cher. Once she started writing, though, she ver stopped. Today she lives in the English ntryside with her five horses, her cat Sugar pe, and her dog Fluffy. Every morning before she starts writing, drinks a big wild strawberry smoothie and reads a good book.

funny, when I think about Danielle Star's bio, she reminds me so many characters that we just happen to olish at Papercutz! For example, she was assistant cook at a famous French pastry op, and that makes me think of SWEETIES, eries published by our Charmz imprint, and sed on *The Chocolate Box Girls* books by thy Cassidy. The series is about a recently nded family, where the dad works as a ndy-maker. Danielle was also involved the world of fashion, something of great erest to BARBIE in her Papercutz graphic vels. She also was a dance teacher, and need I mention that we olish the wonderful DANCE CLASS graphic novels by Bêka and p? But when I saw that Danielle has five horses and a dog named ffy…well, I think I'm beginning to see where she might come with ideas for some of her characters.

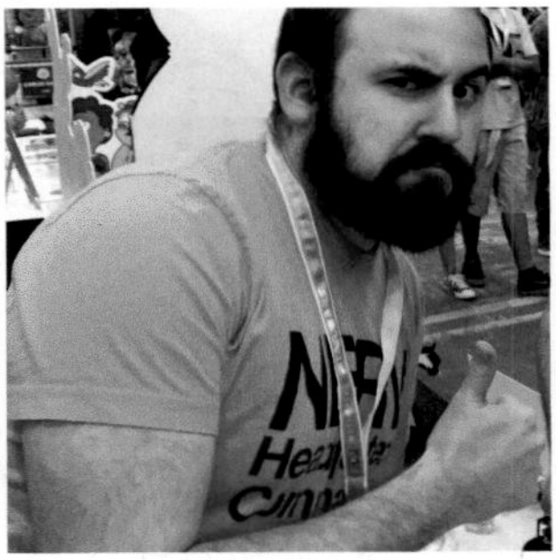

Ryan Jampole

rtney Powell, the writer of the MELOWY graphic novels was born Alabama, but lived most of her life in the magical realm of New rk City. Cortney is a writer, poet, actress, filmmaker, animal-lover, d yogini. At an early age Cortney met Batman co-creator Bob ne and filmmakers Francis Ford Coppola and Lloyd Kaufman at e San Diego Comic-Con. At the prestigious Professional Performing ts School, she was proud to star as Enid in cartoonist/playwright nda Barry's play "The Good Times Are Killing Me." A fan of such comics as BARBIE, LENORE, and LITTLE LULU, Cortney worked on revising the DISNEY FAIRIES scripts for an American audience for the Papercutz graphic novels. Her magical comics journey continues as the writer on the MELOWY graphic novel series, where she believes the most powerful magic of all is: Love.

A yogini, eh? That may offer some insights into why Cora is practicing meditation techniques!

As for MELOWY artist Ryan Jampole, he's quite an accomplished comicbook artist, and has even been nominated for the prestigious Harvey Award, one of the highest honors in the field. Ryan hails from Queens, New York, and attended the High School of Art & Design and the Fashion Institute of Technology—which explains why the fashions showcased by the fashion club were so impressive! Among Ryan's many comics credits, he has drawn MEGAMAN and SONIC for Archie Comics, DEXTER'S LABORATORY and CODENAME KND for IDW, and GEEKY F@B 5, GERONIMO STILTON and THEA STILTON graphic novels for Papercutz.

Speaking of THEA STILTON, we want to mention that her Papercutz graphic novels are being collected in the exciting 3 IN 1 format that's become the latest sensation! It's a simple concept, each 3 IN 1 book collects three entire Papercutz graphic novels into one great big Papercutz graphic novel. In MELOWY #1, we offered a peek at GERONIMO STILTON 3 IN 1 #1, now we'd like to offer a peek into THEA STILTON 3 IN 1 #1 starting on the very next page.

Any discussion of our MELOWY graphic novel creators should also include colorist Laurie E. Smith and letterer Wilson Ramos Jr., but we're running out of room, so we'll have to save their exciting bios until MELOWY #3 "Time to Fly."

Thanks, JIM

STAY IN TOUCH!

EMAIL:	salicrup@papercutz.com
WEB:	papercutz.com
TWITTER:	@papercutzgn
INSTAGRAM:	@papercutzgn
FACEBOOK:	PAPERCUTZGRAPHICNOVELS
FANMAIL:	Papercutz, 160 Broadway, Suite 700, East Wing, New York, NY 10038

Here's a special preview of THEA STILTON 3 IN 1 #1...

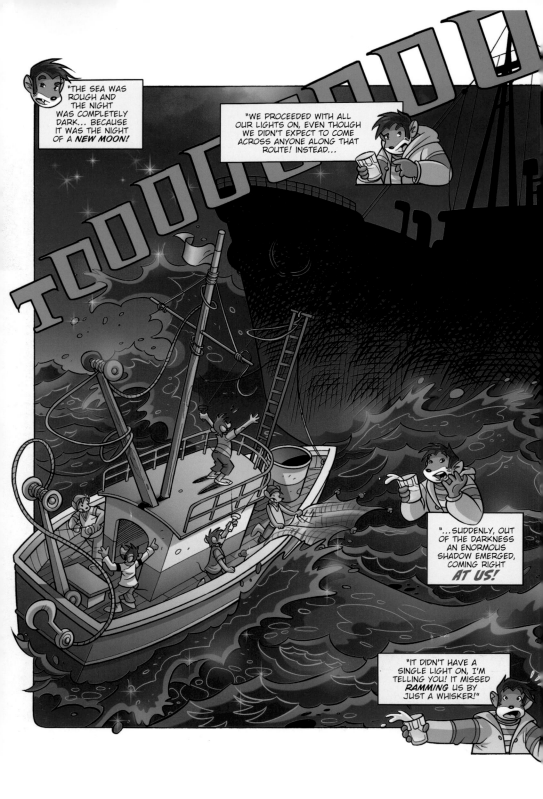

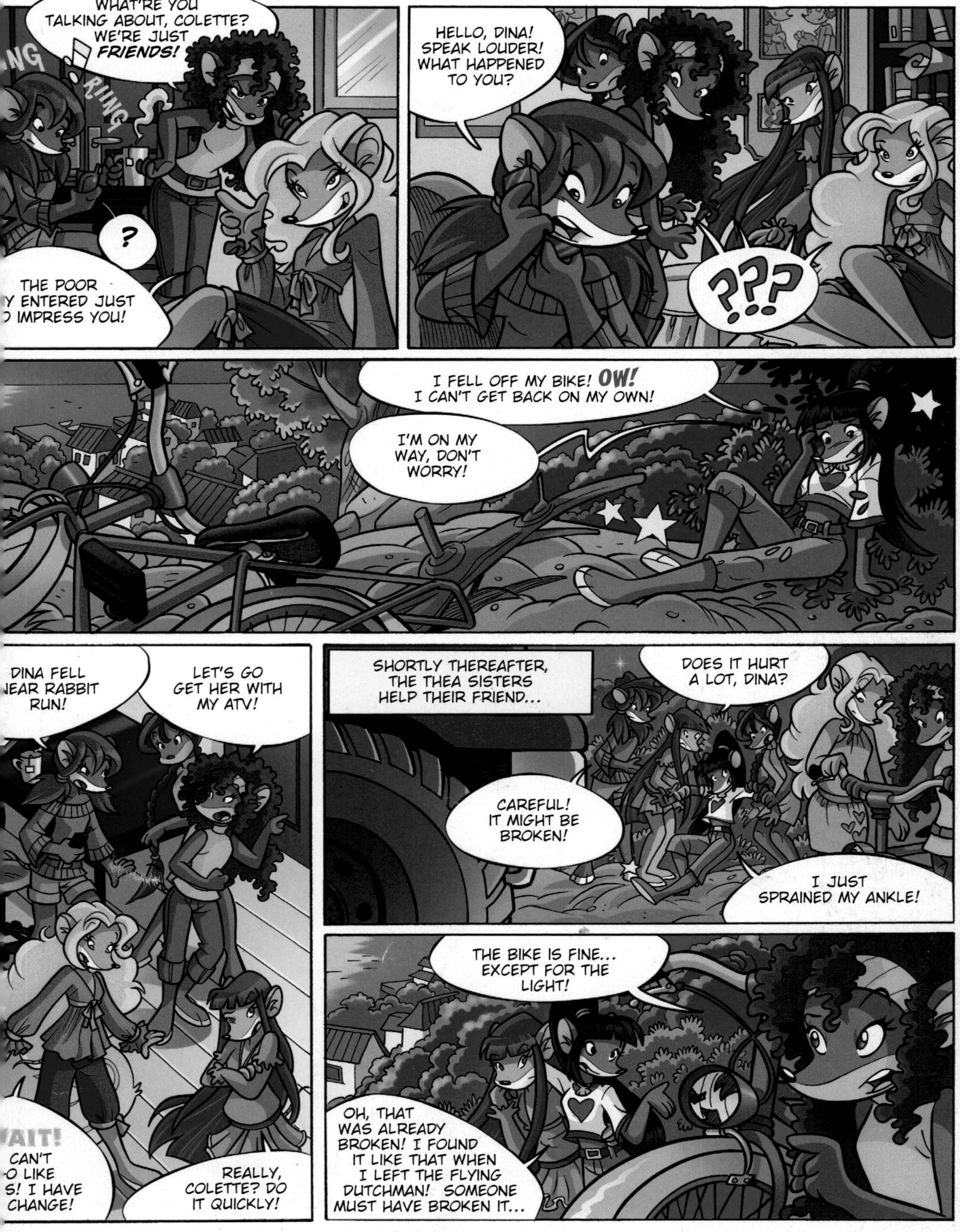

WHAT'RE YOU TALKING ABOUT, COLETTE? WE'RE JUST FRIENDS!
?
THE POOR
Y ENTERED JUST
O IMPRESS YOU!
HELLO, DINA! SPEAK LOUDER! WHAT HAPPENED TO YOU?
???
I FELL OFF MY BIKE! OW! I CAN'T GET BACK ON MY OWN!
I'M ON MY WAY, DON'T WORRY!
DINA FELL
NEAR RABBIT RUN!
LET'S GO GET HER WITH MY ATV!
AIT!
CAN'T
O LIKE
S! I HAVE
CHANGE!
REALLY, COLETTE? DO IT QUICKLY!
SHORTLY THEREAFTER, THE THEA SISTERS HELP THEIR FRIEND...
DOES IT HURT A LOT, DINA?
CAREFUL! IT MIGHT BE BROKEN!
I JUST SPRAINED MY ANKLE!
THE BIKE IS FINE... EXCEPT FOR THE LIGHT!
OH, THAT WAS ALREADY BROKEN! I FOUND IT LIKE THAT WHEN I LEFT THE FLYING DUTCHMAN! SOMEONE MUST HAVE BROKEN IT...

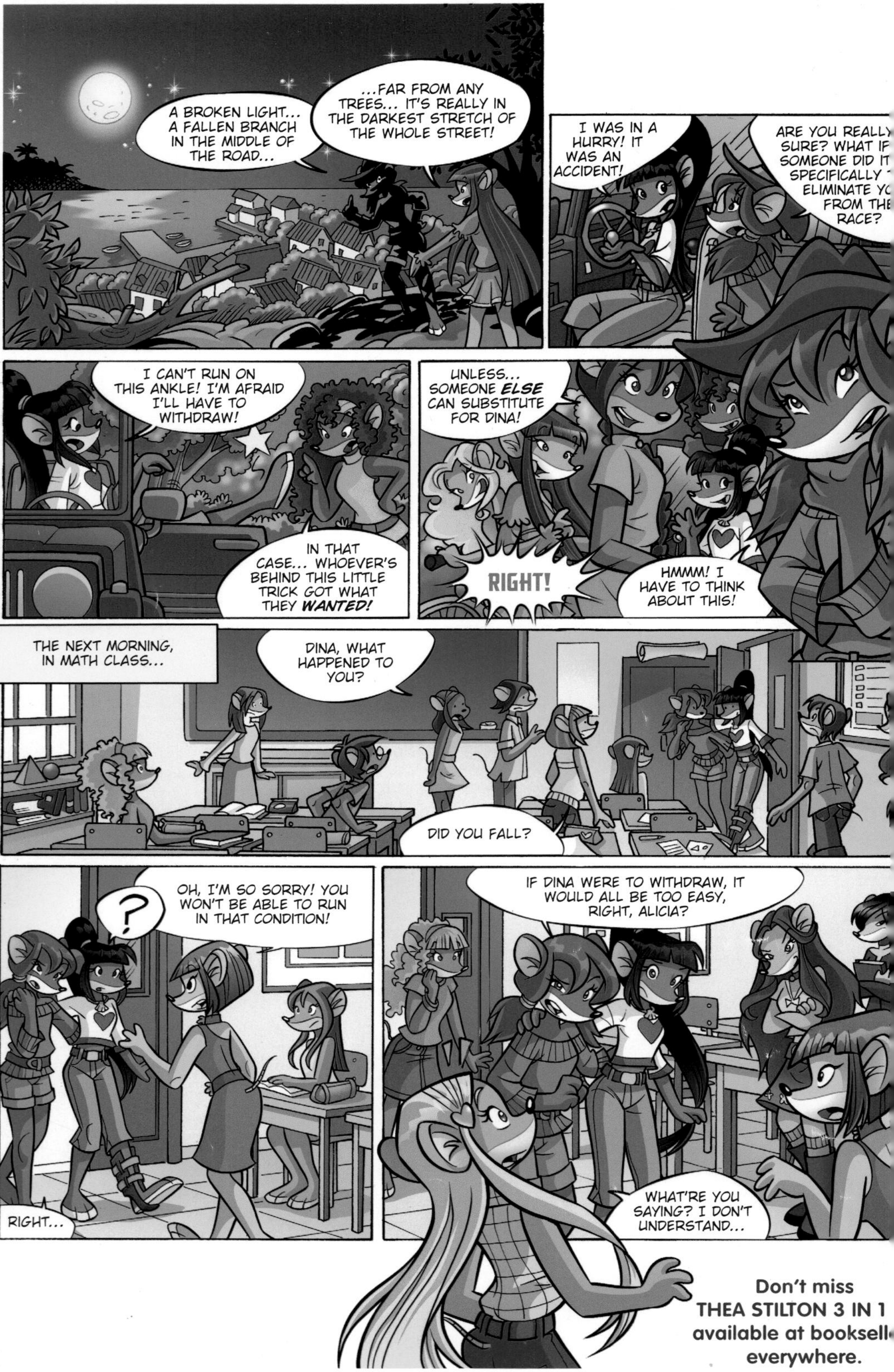
A BROKEN LIGHT... A FALLEN BRANCH IN THE MIDDLE OF THE ROAD...
...FAR FROM ANY TREES... IT'S REALLY IN THE DARKEST STRETCH OF THE WHOLE STREET!
I WAS IN A HURRY! IT WAS AN ACCIDENT!
ARE YOU REALL SURE? WHAT IF SOMEONE DID IT SPECIFICALLY ELIMINATE YO FROM THE RACE?
I CAN'T RUN ON THIS ANKLE! I'M AFRAID I'LL HAVE TO WITHDRAW!
IN THAT CASE... WHOEVER'S BEHIND THIS LITTLE TRICK GOT WHAT THEY *WANTED!*
UNLESS... SOMEONE *ELSE* CAN SUBSTITUTE FOR DINA!
RIGHT!
HMMM! I HAVE TO THINK ABOUT THIS!
THE NEXT MORNING, IN MATH CLASS...
DINA, WHAT HAPPENED TO YOU?
DID YOU FALL?
?
OH, I'M SO SORRY! YOU WON'T BE ABLE TO RUN IN THAT CONDITION!
RIGHT...
IF DINA WERE TO WITHDRAW, IT WOULD ALL BE TOO EASY, RIGHT, ALICIA?
WHAT'RE YOU SAYING? I DON'T UNDERSTAND...

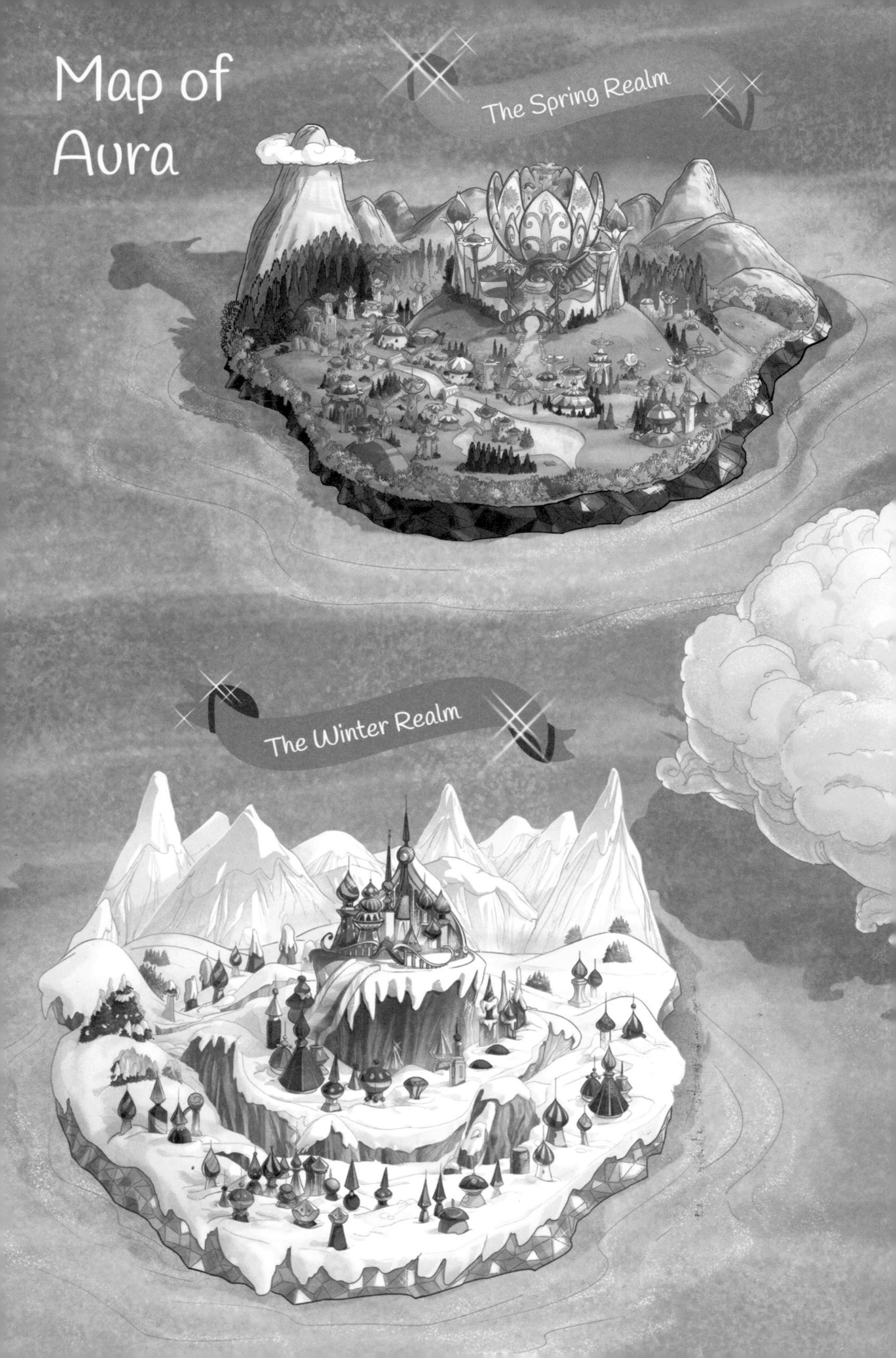
Map of Aura
The Spring Realm
The Winter Realm